CALEB

The K9 Files, Book 11

Dale Mayer

Books in This Series:

Ethan, Book 1
Pierce, Book 2
Zane, Book 3
Blaze, Book 4
Lucas, Book 5
Parker, Book 6
Carter, Book 7
Weston, Book 8
Greyson, Book 9
Rowan, Book 10
Caleb, Book 11
Kurt, Book 12

CALEB: THE K9 FILES, BOOK 11
Dale Mayer
Valley Publishing Ltd.

Copyright © 2020

All rights reserved. Except for use in any review, the reproduction or utilization of this work in whole or in part by any electronic, mechanical or other means, now known or hereafter invented, including xerography, photocopying and recording, or in any information storage or retrieval system, is forbidden without the written permission of the publisher.

This is a work of fiction. Names, characters, places, brands, media, and incidents are either the product of the author's imagination or are used fictitiously. Any resemblance to actual events, locales, or persons, living or dead, is entirely coincidental.

ISBN-13: 978-1-773363-15-8
Print Edition

About This Book

Welcome to the all new K9 Files series reconnecting readers with the unforgettable men from SEALs of Steel in a new series of action packed, page turning romantic suspense that fans have come to expect from USA TODAY Bestselling author Dale Mayer. Pssst… you'll meet other favorite characters from SEALs of Honor and Heroes for Hire too!

For Caleb, returning to his hometown for his brother's wedding should have been cause for a wonderful celebration. However, since his brother is marrying Caleb's ex-wife, Caleb doesn't want to go anywhere near the event. Yet Caleb returns, as his best friend, Laysha, is in the same town, and they are overdue a reunion. Plus Caleb's been asked to look into a War Dog adopted out but now missing.

Having Caleb back in town, at her house even, Laysha couldn't be happier, all the while knowing Caleb still had issues with his ex-wife. When Caleb and Laysha take a trip to the last known residence where the War Dog had been and instead find a human corpse, life takes a dark turn.

Even worse, they are seen at the house and have both become targets … in a game Caleb has to win or will lose everything that's important in his life.

PROLOGUE

BADGER SAT AT the Titanium Corp boardroom table with the whole original crew—Erick, Cade, Talon, Laszlo, Geir, and Jager—which was unusual. Badger said, "Did I just hear that Rowan is coming back to New Mexico with Brandi?"

"Yep. The whole crew. Including War Dog Hershey and Brandi's Lab, Lacey, with her three puppies, which I don't know if they have names for yet," Geir said. "Talk about a happy ending."

Talon shook his head. "We're getting damn good at this, aren't we?"

Badger chuckled. "And trust you to take the credit for something like this," he said.

"What do you mean?" Erick asked. "We've all done a hell of a job."

"Maybe so," Badger said, "but the bottom line is, these couples worked it out themselves, and that's what matters."

"And the War Dogs get a whole new life," Cade said.

"A whole new life but also a family," Badger said. "That's the best part. Not only is Hershey back with Rowan, but Hershey will have a perfect retirement now."

"We'll get to see them too," Kat said, as she walked in. "I'm looking forward to meeting Brandi."

"Why is that?" Jager asked.

"She's into stem cells," she said. "I want to talk to her about rejuvenating some of the scar tissue at amputation sites." She gave Badger a sweet, yet sexy, tilt of her head. "You know there could be an awful lot of benefit to having her around."

The men looked at her, as Badger wrapped an arm around his wife, kissed her on the temple, and said, "That's Kat for you. She always wants to make our lives better."

"Hey, you can't argue against that," she said, turning to wrap her arms around him.

He reached a hand down and patted her belly. "In case you guys hadn't heard the news."

Immediately the guys jumped up and gave her hugs.

"We're pretty thrilled," she said, "but we've still got more War Dogs here that need checking up on."

"We do," Badger said. "Plus the commander contacted me, and he said that we've done such a hell of a job that he's wondering if we can take on a few more cases."

The men looked at him in shock.

"We're not done with the ones we have yet," Laszlo said.

"I know. I do know that," Badger said. "So we've got to finish these jobs and then maybe take another look at what we want to do. He's got a few more cases for us."

"I'm game," Geir said.

"Agreed," said Talon, the rest nodding. "So what have we got?"

Geir pulled one of the two remaining original War Dogs folders closer to him and flipped it open.

"And what's with that one?" Erick asked, sipping his coffee.

"Texas," he said. "He's at the El Paso border."

"And what? The dog has gone to Mexico?" Cade glanced

at all the men gathered here.

"We have no idea," Geir noted. "It was there with a family one day, and, the next day, he was gone."

Laszlo asked, "Kidnapped, coyotes, shot, what?"

"No clue," Badger said. "Do we have anybody we can send?"

"Me." The voice came from the doorway, and they looked over to see Caleb walk in.

"You've got a connection to Texas?" Badger asked.

"I do," he said. "Family down there. Where in Texas?"

"Not too far away from El Paso," Geir said.

"A good friend has a big place down there, lots of land."

"Not a whole lot grows there, does it?" Talon asked.

"No, it takes a lot of land to make a living," he said. "But, she bought it for the peace and quiet."

"Are they down by the border?" Geir asked.

"Both sides of the border actually," he said. "What's the deal with the dog?"

"Not a whole lot to tell you," Geir said, reading the file quickly. "It was adopted by a family, and, when the government did the first check, the dog had already disappeared."

"Was it a runner?"

"It never used to be," Badger said. "You want to go down and find out?"

"Oh, yeah," Caleb said. "I do."

"You got a hidden reason for going?" Talon asked.

"Not hiding anything," Caleb said. "I'm going down for my brother's wedding."

"Oh, good," Kat said. "I love hearing about weddings."

But Caleb's face darkened. "Not this one," he said.

"Why is that?" she asked.

"Because he's marrying my ex-wife."

CHAPTER 1

CALEB DANSWORTH WALKED out of the airport and headed toward the rental cars, when he heard his name called. He turned and stopped in surprise as Lazy—or Laysha, her real name—raced toward him. He opened his arms at the last moment, as she threw herself into them. He laughed, hugged her tight, and swung her off her feet, before putting her down again. "I didn't expect to see you," he said.

"I sent you a text, saying I'd pick you up," she said, "but I know that you wanted a rental vehicle."

"I hate not having wheels," he admitted.

"And I didn't want you to pay for wheels if you weren't hanging around for long," she said stepping back, but her gaze searched his.

He reached out gently, stroked her cheek. "Damn, it's good to see you, Lazy."

"And don't call me by that nickname," she said, holding up a hand.

"Lazy?" he asked with a lopsided grin. "Man, we made your life hell over that nickname, didn't we?"

"Yes," she said, chuckling. "So what's it to be? Do you want to come home with me or do you want to stop and pick up a rental?"

He frowned at that.

"You can get a rental in town, if you find you need it,"

she said. "I can always drive you there later."

"I have to cancel the one I have on order."

"Do it now then," she said. "No point spending any money if you don't have to."

He knew where she was coming from because they spent a lot of time growing up without any money. Plus, she knew what he'd been through this last year—or at least a little bit of it. In response, he pulled out his phone, brought up the app he had used, and quickly cancelled the rental car. He wasn't sure if there'd be a penalty for that, but, at this point in time, he didn't really care.

She laughed, hooked her arm through his, and said, "Come on. Let's go."

"You're looking good," he said, eyeing the leggy blonde beside him, like he hadn't really done before. "But then you always look good."

"Ha," she said, tossing him that big grin that he remembered so well. "If I looked that good, you'd have come back and visited me more."

He snorted. "I had a lot of reasons for not coming back."

She nodded slowly. "Sorry about that."

"And yet you wanted me to come for the wedding. Why is that again?" he asked, hating what lay ahead.

"Because it's holding you back," she said immediately.

"Like hell," he snapped.

"Yep. The minute you find something that you don't want to do," she said, "you know you have to face it."

"No, I really don't."

"You do. You love your brother."

"Which is why I told him to run when he hooked up with her."

She stared at him in shock. "Did you really?"

"Of course I did," he said. "As you said, I love my brother. That woman's a viper."

"I have to admit she does seem a little different now from when she was married to you. Not that I knew her enough to really tell. Once you married her, I didn't want to be around you two."

That twisted in his gut too. "So maybe I was the wrong man for her," he said shortly. "But that doesn't mean the treatment I got from her was deserved either."

"Nope, it wasn't," Laysha said. "But it is what it is."

"Yep, I'm with you there."

"Besides," she said, tossing him a sidelong look as they dashed across the road, heading for a parking lot farther out, "it's been four years since the divorce. Surely you're over her by now?"

"I am," he said. "I mean, I've been divorced longer than I was married."

"Yeah, a time measurement that makes it easier, doesn't it?"

"What about you? You were married for a couple years in there too?"

"Yep, I sure was," she said, as she scrunched up her face. "And I'm glad that's over too."

"So what the hell is wrong with us that we get married, think it's the best thing ever, and then, a few years later, we can't wait to get out of it?"

"Because it wasn't right to begin with."

"I'm not sure I'll ever believe in that whole getting-married-again scenario," he said. "I really didn't think marrying Sarah would be a bad deal."

"And I didn't think marrying Paul would be a bad deal," she said, "but I'm not sure either of us married for the right reasons."

"Well, I married fast because I was going back out on missions," he said, "so I'll give you that."

"Exactly," she said, "so you didn't give the relationship a long enough time to figure out if that's who she really was."

"Maybe, but I also thought she was pregnant with my baby."

"Yeah, I heard about that," she said with a nod. She pointed across the parking lot. "I'm over there at the far end." They turned in that direction. "Apparently she lost it soon after you got married?"

"I wasn't in town," he said, "but yes."

"And then you found out it wasn't even yours?"

"True. And, of course, after that, there's … well it's pretty hard to get the relationship back on track."

"Did you ever think that maybe she was terrified and was just looking for somebody to help out?"

"Then she should have said that," he snapped.

She nodded. "I definitely agree with that."

"Besides," he said, "I tried hard, but, to know that she already tried to pass off my … somebody else's baby as mine, well …"

"But you didn't know that right away, did you?"

"No. Not right away. Not until we had a couple fights, and she threw it in my face."

"Did she ever tell you whose baby it was?"

"No," he said. "I asked her, but she never did tell me."

"But you didn't know originally it wasn't yours?"

"Nope, I didn't," he said. "I'm just a fool. I wanted to believe …"

"That just makes you a good man," she said, patting his arm.

"I don't know," he said. "After I found out what she'd done, I wasn't a very good guy about it at all."

"But that's a human response to betrayal though, right?"

"I know," he said, "and it wasn't very much fun to live through."

"Still, it's past time now to deal with it."

"Yeah." He stopped. They had reached her truck. He looked at her and said, "Did you ever hear anything about it?"

"Not a whole lot, mostly the little bit you told me," she said.

"Yeah, and that was a while ago."

"I did hear a few more rumors since then," she said.

Something in her tone had him looking at her in surprise. "Like what?"

She sighed. "I don't know if I should tell you."

"Tell me," he said in a hard voice. "Nothing about this is easy."

"She mentioned that the baby she lost when she was married to you was actually your brother's."

LAYSHA ARKANSAS LOOKED over at the man she had always loved to see his reaction to that news. He just stared at her in shock. She winced. She pulled her keys from her pocket, quickly unlocked the truck, and said, "Come on. Get in." She watched and yet tried to ignore his stricken expression on his face as he moved to the passenger side and slowly got in her truck. She turned on the engine and pivoted to face him. "I thought you should know."

He looked at her, still wordless.

"I know," she said. "I know. All kinds of ramifications come from this." She sat here, hoping he would talk about it.

"You're not kidding," he said, his voice harsh. "Was I cuckolded from the entire get-go?"

"You already know the answer to that," she said. "It wasn't your baby anyway. Now you know who the father was."

"And my brother? Did they carry this on the whole time I was married to her?"

"I hope not," Laysha said. "I would hope that you and your brother have a better relationship than that."

"Well, I thought so," he said, "but you're making me wonder." He turned, looked out the passenger window.

"Then ask him about it, while you're here, and clear the air," she said, "because nothing is worse than worrying in the background about it all."

"It sucks," he said, then finally focused on her. "And I had no idea. Or is she just saying that to throw a wrench in the works?"

"And that's possible too. Your brother was out of town for quite a few years. Remember that?"

"So maybe they split up, and then she latched on to me?"

"I wouldn't be at all surprised," she said, "and I get that you probably hate her for everything that went on, but don't let her destroy you."

He lifted one eyebrow and cocked his head at her.

She laughed. "Yeah, okay. She has this ugly side, yet surely something about her must be redeeming? Your brother loves her."

"You think so?" he said. He shook his head, fastening his seat belt. "You think whatever you want to think," he said.

"Right now I don't have a clue how to interpret that news."

"And that's why I suggest you talk to them about it."

"Do they know I'm coming in for the wedding? And only the wedding? That's more than enough without having to attend the rehearsal too."

"Well, your brother did want you for his best man, but I hear you turned down that role?"

"Yeah, I didn't want to be around her any more than I had to be."

"I think your brother does understand that. At least somewhat. I think he's also hoping to make peace."

"Maybe. I don't know that a whole lot of peace can be made between him and me. Although maybe, … maybe I'm the fool here. Maybe they've been the real item, and I was just the baggage along the way."

"Well, let's not worry about it," she said, settling in the driver's seat, clicking her seat belt into place. "What's this about a War Dog?"

He looked at her for a moment, and she saw him visibly try to pull back from his brother and all the emotions entailed in that. He took a long slow deep breath. "Beowulf. At least that's his nickname. His legal name is a series of names. He's a trained War Dog but was released to retire."

She quickly drove through the parking lot, punching her ticket into the machine, paying the tab via her phone, and then pulled out onto the main highway, heading home. "And that's got what to do with you?"

"It's hard to say. It's more a case of, I'll do what I can do. If I pick up his trail, then I'll carry on. He came to an adopted family, and they let him out to go to the bathroom the next morning, and he never came back."

She stared at him and then returned her gaze to the road.

"So he was only there for one night? Was it that bad?"

"Or was it not fenced? Did he get taken by somebody else or did the coyotes get him, whether human or animal? Or did he try to head back home, looking for the war where he spent all those years?" he said. "It's really hard to know."

"And do you have a picture of him?"

"I do," he said. "It's in my bag. He looks like a really stocky black shepherd. The only other color on him is a brown and black pattern found on his ears."

"Interesting," she murmured. "Well, I certainly haven't seen any dog like it."

"The only thing I have to go on is the place he went missing from."

"And how long ago?'

"It's been a couple months now."

"Well, that's a useless trip then, isn't it?"

"Maybe," he said, "I don't really know yet."

"I'm sorry," she said, "but at least it brought you here."

"It did. I'm not so sure I'm happy about that right now though."

She nodded slowly. "Well, if nothing else," she said, "I am delighted to see you."

He barked out a laugh at that. "And I missed you too," he said affectionately.

She shook her head. "But not enough to come back and visit, huh?"

"Nope," he said. "Since the divorce, I buried myself in work. Then was injured and haven't come up for air since." He added, "And then it became a habit."

"Will you stop living just because of her?"

"Well, I was hoping not to repeat my mistake," he said jokingly.

She smiled and nodded. As she headed home, she wondered how to broach the conversation. But then he said it himself.

"What about you?" he asked. "You planning to marry again?"

CHAPTER 2

LAYSHA NODDED. "I hope so," she said. "I married basically after feeling rejected by somebody I really cared about. Threw myself into that substitute relationship and honestly don't feel like I did Paul any service. The divorce was a relief for both of us. I did try to make it work, but you can't force feelings that don't exist."

"Good point," he said. After an awkward pause, he looked at her several times, as if wanting to ask a question.

She didn't offer anything, focusing on the traffic instead. "How will you figure out where the dog went from here?"

"Well, that's another reason I need wheels," he said. "I'll go to the last place he was and see what I can figure out."

"And why would somebody take the dog?"

"Jealousy? There's quite a vetting process to adopt a War Dog after it's been retired from service."

"But then somebody else could have just applied and been given another one," she said.

"True. And maybe it ran away because it didn't like something about the scenario. Don't forget these dogs are highly trained, but they've also been through tough times. They can come back with PTSD, just like the human soldiers do.

"In some ways they need to be retrained to enter their civilian life of retirement, just like for me and others like me who were injured. I have his file, and I've read some of it, and he'd gone through several handlers before his retirement, after which several said he was difficult to work with. Mostly over his attachment to his one handler who died on the job. He was trained to find bombs and other chemical weapons."

"So was Beowulf aggressive? Maybe he did something really ugly, like attacking the adopting couple's children or something, and the owner shot him and buried him, thinking good riddance?" She shivered. "But I hope not. All dogs deserve a second chance."

"The couple had no kids," he said, "and Beowulf's file doesn't show any aggressive tendency, other than when called into action. However, that's certainly a possibility, although it's not the one I want to hear."

"Well, we're almost there, at home," she said, as she switched from city roads to country roads, and finally turned on her signal to pull into her driveway.

"You sure you're okay with me staying with you?"

She looked at him in surprise. "Why not?" she asked. "You've stayed with me lots."

"I know, but I used to stay with my brother a lot of times too."

"Well, you can stay with him if you want," she said. "You know your ex-wife's there."

"True. That's ... that's a good enough reason to keep me away."

"But you do *you*," she said. She hopped out, closed the truck door, and headed to her front porch. She knew he had come up behind her as she turned to open the door and let her dogs out. Three dogs raced outside, barking like crazy, as if they'd just been attacked, and headed toward him. He dropped his big duffel bag and bent down to say hi to them.

Immediately they turned into the slobberiest pups ever. She shook her head as she watched them. "Every damn time you're here," she said, "you can make the biggest, strongest, baddest animal turn into Jell-O."

He chuckled. "They know I'm a softy inside," he said, trying to pet all three of them, as they wiggled in his hands.

"Says you," she said. "Graynor's inside on the couch."

"You still got him?"

"Not for much longer," she said sadly. "He's fifteen and well past his time."

He nodded in empathy. "And there's nothing quite like losing our canine friends, is there?"

"Well, losing family's worse, yet he's furry family," she said. She walked in and called out, "Graynor, somebody to see you." She could hear the *thump* of his tail on the couch. She walked around. She had blankets laid out for him, and here her great big old German wirehaired pointer was stretched out on the cushions with his eyes open, not moving, except for his tail wiggling. She bent down, gave him a quick cuddle and a kiss, and then stepped back so he saw Caleb. Immediately he struggled to get to his feet.

Caleb stepped forward. "Hey, old man, stay where you are. It's okay." And he dropped to his knees to cuddle the huge dog that he had known since Graynor was a pup.

The two connected like long-lost friends, and it brought tears to Laysha's eyes because she knew she would lose Graynor at some point, and she wasn't ready for it. She would never be ready for that. He had been there for her through the thick and the thin, through fifteen years of her life. Half of it. Almost half of it. She would be thirty next month. And here that guy had been a birthday gift for her after she had rescued him, but then her parents had refused to let her keep him. She had cried for days and weeks after they took him away, and finally they decided that she could have him and brought him back to her for her birthday gift. She and Graynor had been inseparable ever since. But she knew that, even though he had had a good life with her, his time was coming to an end.

She walked into the kitchen, more to control the choking in the back of her throat, and she put on coffee, staring out the window to focus on something happier.

She had five acres of land here. The one thing that she had really prided herself on when she needed to buy a house was *space*. She had lived in apartments, small townhomes, and everything possible in a city that made her feel cramped and too close to her neighbors. When she finally bought her own place, she purchased a house just out of the city and managed to get five acres with it, although not a whole lot grew on it. It took the bulk of her money to get it fenced, and she did most of that herself.

She smiled at the memory. The house was by no means new, but it was hers.

The old farmhouse needed a lot of upgrades, but something was extremely comforting about the original residence that had lasted as long as it had. As she looked up, Caleb walked toward her.

"This farmhouse," he said with a shake of his head, "it still looks the same."

"Yeah," she said with a nod. "Takes money and time to fix it up, and I just haven't got to a whole lot of it."

"No, but I did see new boards on the front veranda," he said in a mild tone.

"And that's a new faucet." She laughed. "Yeah, some of the plumbing had to be redone," she said. "After the fence, it was plumbing and electrical. The rest of it's cosmetic," she said with a wave of her hand, "and I can live with most of it." She looked at the wallpaper, laughed, and said, "Although this wallpaper has to go."

He groaned. "It's still the same, isn't it?" He reached out a hand to touch it; it was half raised velveteen in an orange and brown brocade pattern. "God, who would have put something like this in the kitchen?"

"I don't know," she said. "Coffee's on. Let's take a cup to the back veranda." And she pushed open the big slider door and stepped out.

He smiled as he joined her and said, "Honestly the best thing about this old farmhouse," he said, "is the wraparound veranda. You never find porches anywhere like this anymore."

"And I love it," she said. "There was a lot to fall in love with here. But it's taking more time than I thought to get it to the point where I thought it would be by now."

"It's just you doing the rehab," he said, "and a single paycheck to fund these projects. Not to mention the hours at the day job where you get said paycheck. At least you managed to hang on to this gem when you were married."

"I rented it during that time," she said. "Paul didn't like the farmhouse at all. That should have been a huge red flag for me."

"But that's not why you married," he said. "You married for the companionship and to make sure you weren't an old maid, right?"

Startled, she stared at him. "Well, I'd hate to even think of it in those terms," she said, "but a certain amount of truth is in those words, yes. I certainly married because I didn't want to be alone anymore," she said, "so that's part of it."

"And it's hard," he said. "We want so much for ourselves. And then we turn around, and it's all changed, and it's different, and all those plans that you made? They go out the window." He stopped and stared, as he looked back at the clapboard siding and the big old windows. "Instead of replacing the windows, you could probably get a secondary layer of glass added."

She nodded. "And I actually have a quote for it too somewhere," she said. "I'll start at one side of one floor and then move along," she said, "but the fence took way more than I thought, then the plumbing became an issue."

"How's the plumbing now?"

"It's fine," she said. "I've completely redone the upstairs en suite bathroom and the downstairs guest bathroom," she said, "because it's just a little powder room. The upstairs guest bathroom still needs work, but it's got a new bathtub and a new toilet. I haven't got the vanity installed yet."

"Are you still doing all the work yourself?"

"No, not all of it," she said. "I contracted some of it out. I'm not that great with plumbing, and I really suck at electrical."

He grinned. He looped an arm around her shoulders, tucked her up close, and said, "You're the only person I know with as many skills as you have, and yet you still think you suck."

"I'm a fair hand with wood," she said. "I can fix anything, and I could probably install the glass myself, but I still have to order the glass to fit, and generally they don't just let you have the glass to install it yourself."

"It depends whether you have to pull out these existing glass windows and reinstall them only because you don't have enough room to work with," he said, dropping his arm from her shoulders and walking to the window. He tested the bottom panel and nodded. "You know what? I think you could probably install them yourself."

"I was thinking about it," she said. "I just haven't got that far yet. It would cut the price in half."

He looked at her and said, "I don't know if you can afford the cost of the glass now, but, while I'm here, I'm happy to help do something. I'm not sure what your priority is. Just let me know."

"How are your tiling skills?" she said with a cheeky grin. "I've got that new vanity to put in the guest bathroom and tiles to set."

"Well, we've set more than a few tiles ourselves," he said. "So why not? Have you got them?"

She nodded with a big grin and said, "Come on. I'll show you." And she raced up the stairs ahead of him.

"THIS IS THE Laysha who I remember," he murmured to himself, as he followed her, taking a big sip of coffee so he didn't spill it as he went. He hadn't told her how much he loved this farmhouse, but it was to die for. It was massive. It was old. The heating needed some work. But thankfully they were in Texas, so it's not like it was as bad as if they lived farther north. The fact that she had five acres here made it a deal as far as he was concerned. She bought it before he even knew about it.

When she told him what she had done, he wholeheartedly approved and was half jealous that he hadn't found it first. He might have moved back home if he had a place like this to come to. As it was, she had helped him on a bunch of renovations that he had been doing on his brother's house years ago, plus on his own house at the time—which he then sold during the divorce—so it was only fair that he helped her on a few of hers.

As he walked into the upstairs guest bathroom, he whistled. "Wow," he said, "you're really taking this old girl and moving her into the new century."

"Just because she's old," Laysha said, "doesn't mean she doesn't deserve the best."

A beautiful bathtub, a big clawfoot, modernized with stand-up plumbing on the outside of it, sat in front of a huge window that overlooked her acreage. The floor underneath had been tiled right up to where the bathtub rested, but the remainder of the tiling hadn't been done, and a walk-in shower was off on one side, built into a small section, all the tiling completed in there—loved that, complete with the great big rain showerhead. He noted the vanity sitting here but not installed. "You've done a lot of this work," he said, "and it looks fantastic."

"Well, it was really selfish of me," she said, "but I did the en suite first. So now this guest bath needs the vanity set and the tiling done," she added, "and then it's pretty good to go."

"Show me the en suite." As he headed across the hallway, he realized that the master took half the upstairs, and the other half comprised the two smaller guest bedrooms sharing that guest bathroom. As he walked into her bedroom, he whistled. "I forgot how big this was."

It had a big arched ceiling and huge semicircle windows on both sides. And she had a massive queen bed in the center, piled high with bedding. It looked so damn inviting that he had to stop and stare for a moment.

"Problems?" she asked from the corner. He turned,

looked at her, motioned to the bed, and said, "Damn, that looks good."

"I didn't even remake it this morning," she confessed. "Normally I do. I just tossed the covers today though."

"Yeah, well, I've been traveling for a little bit too long," he said, "and that looks pretty damn fine to me." He walked over to the open en suite bath and stared. "Wow." A huge walk-in shower, with three sets of jets and a bench seat, sat next to a big bathtub, very similar to the other clawfoot tub, only a step higher. Plus, all the tiling been done halfway up on the walls all the way around. "Damn, you do good work."

"It took a lot of man-hours," she said. "I only finished it about two months ago."

"There's no *only* about it." As he turned, he looked and said, "Hardwood floors, right?"

"Yes. I stripped and refinished them before I moved in the bed," she said. "I stayed in the spare room until I had it done."

"Is this room done then?"

"It is," she said. "These windows are already doubled. They were cracked when I bought the place, so I had to replace them. Those are all new. And I haven't done anything about upgrading the insulation in the roof yet," she said, "but I might."

"Where's the attic, and is it something you can do yourself, or will you need to spray it in?"

"The attic is just a cutaway access hole right now, but spray in would be easier for insulating it," she said. With that, they headed back downstairs, going room by room, as he noted things that needed to be done and things that they could do without. As he stepped into the original kitchen, he said, "You're such a cook that I figured you'd have redone the kitchen first."

"I wanted to live in it and to figure out what I wanted first," she said. "And I was pretty stressed after the divorce, so I wanted my bedroom done to give me that sanctuary to go to when life got to be too much."

"How's work?"

"It's okay," she said. She was a paralegal, and her days at work were the complete opposite of what she did at home. "It's just always so stressful with all the court-mandated deadlines and the fear of making a single typo that can undo a whole contract."

"It's that type of job, isn't it?"

"It is. The lawyers make the big money, and we do all the grunt work," she said with a laugh. "I should have finished law school."

"You should have," he said.

She rolled her eyes at him. "No more of that I-told-you-so stuff, please."

"Nah," he said, "besides, you already know. *I told you so.*"

She laughed at that. "Right," she said, "that was your one and only freebie."

He grinned, refilled his coffee, and stepped back out on the porch. "Damn, I love this place."

"Me too," she said. She walked up, poked her arm through his elbow, and said, "I'm glad you're here for a few days."

"Maybe a little longer," he said, "but, if I'm an inconvenience, I can go to a hotel."

She stared at him in shock. "No way," she said. "Besides, I need help here."

He laughed. "From what I can see, you're doing just fine

on your own."

"It's so strange," she said, shaking her head. "It's one of those fun things that we did together that I don't know when it ever became something more than a hobby."

"That's because we like to do things with our hands."

"You got me into that," she said in a teasing manner. "How many hours did I spend in the workshop with you?"

"We built some pretty crazy things," he said, grinning. "Yep, we sure did." Just then his phone rang.

She dropped her hand and stepped away so he could pull out his phone.

He frowned as he answered it and said, "Hey, Badger. I'm here."

"Good," Badger said. "Just checking in that you arrived safe and sound."

"Yep, I'm here safe and sound," he said. "Haven't had a chance to check out where the dog went missing from yet though."

"That's fine," he said. "The owners apparently moved."

"Which owners?"

"The ones who took possession of the dog. They've moved into town."

"Interesting," he said. "Well, I still need to get back to the old place where the dog disappeared."

"And you'll have easy access because it's for sale, and nobody's living there," Badger said.

"Did the owners say why they moved?"

"His wife didn't like the country living."

"So why did they want a dog then?"

"Maybe she thought it would make her feel safer. I don't know," Badger said. "We can't ever count on what people think."

When he hung up, Caleb nodded. "Strange."

"What's that?" Laysha said lightly from beside him. He explained what happened with the family. "So maybe they got rid of the dog so that they could move into town and not deal with him? Because no way you could take a big dog like that to live in a small apartment."

"All they had to do was refuse it," he said. "A long list of people want to adopt a War Dog."

She shrugged. "Save face maybe? Or maybe they were involved in something they had to get out of—fast."

"Well, I'll get the couple's current address from Badger." And he quickly sent Badger a request. "I'll talk to the family, and then I will follow up on their original place of residence."

"Well, I've got the next few days off because of all the overtime I'm owed," she said, "so, if you want anybody to ride along, let me know."

CHAPTER 3

LATER THAT EVENING Laysha walked into the kitchen to see Caleb sitting at the table on his phone again. She raised an eyebrow. He smiled, put the phone down, and said, "The rental truck is being delivered in an hour."

"Good," she said. "You ready for dinner then?" And she lifted a basketful of fresh veggies she had pulled from her garden.

He grinned. "Absolutely," he said. "I'll probably take a drive out tonight, although I might leave it until early in the morning."

"You do you," she said comfortably, as she walked into the kitchen and filled the sink with the basket of vegetables. She washed the carrots and the fresh lettuce that she had.

Caleb noticed that she also had two steaks marinating. "Do you want me to light the barbecue?"

"Please do," she said. She quickly prepped the veggies, including chopping bell peppers to go into a big salad. She also had a tin foil packet of sliced potatoes, and, as soon as the barbecue was up to temperature, she put them on first.

"This brings back a lot of memories too."

"Used to be a lot more than just the two of us back then," she said.

"But I like it just being the two of us," he said. "It's the good part about the group back then."

"That's because the group back then included a lot of crazy people."

"I know," he said with a sad smile. "Times change though, don't they?"

"They absolutely do." She smiled. "I'm happy being alone."

"Are you?" he said in surprise. "You always looked to be somebody who liked people."

"Yep, I do like people," she said, "but, at some point in time, you also realize that you aren't really who you are meant to be until you have spent time alone to figure out who that is."

"Now that's deep," he said with a grin.

"Maybe." She shrugged, thoroughly enjoying having him back in her world again. She knew it wouldn't be for long, and he certainly wouldn't stay just because she asked him to. And no point in asking him to because it was not where his heart lay.

Not long thereafter, as she sat down to a hot-off-the-grill barbecued steak, she lifted her glass of wine and said, "To us."

He immediately picked up his glass and echoed her cheer. "I forgot," he said, looking around, "how I feel when I'm here."

"Because it's easier than remembering," she said.

He looked at her, startled.

"Then remembering the hard parts." She shrugged and continued, "I went through the same thing. I walked away from so much of what was important to me because I thought what I was creating was more important. Instead it was just different. And walking away was easier because going back hurt. Plus, it seemed like I'd spent so much time and energy to walk away from what I'd had that it didn't make any sense to go back to it."

"And how does it feel now?" he asked curiously.

"It feels right," she said. "As if I had walked away from something that I shouldn't have, and I'm grateful to circle back here, to have it again now."

He studied her, slowly nodded. "Maybe that's what this trip is all about," he said. "If Jackson and Sarah are happy together, should I hold it against them? No. Obviously your news startled me, and I'm glad to know it ahead of time," he rushed to say, "but it does give me something to think about that I had hoped not to."

"Well, how quickly you deal with it will also tell you how much you actually care about it," she murmured.

He nodded slowly. "And again, something I hadn't really thought about."

"Nope. But that's the … the troublesome part of all this, isn't it?" she said. "We tend to get into a rut, and we think that we're done, but we really aren't."

He laughed. "No hardship in being here with you right now," he said. "I have to tell you that."

"We were best friends," she said, "and I'm so happy to see you now."

"Did you have a bunch of friends from that era, or did you get a new friend group after your marriage broke up?" he asked.

She gave him a lopsided grin. "No, everybody from the past had moved on. I'd separated because it was the right thing to do, and everybody else had their new worlds. People were getting married. People were moving away," she said. "The old group wasn't there anymore. And then, of course, when I did get divorced, nobody understood, and nobody seemed to realize what was going on. I think we made some people uncomfortable, and the friends he had before we got married, he still had, whereas I didn't," she said. "So, when I came back to my old home, this house," she said, "I started all over again. I was alone, and I didn't really know what to do about it at first."

"I think that's part of that whole acclimation process, isn't it? Because I didn't come back anymore as well. I moved out, put everything in storage, and it's still in storage," he said with a shrug. "And I've done as much overtime work as I can. Times off, I travel."

"You always had the travel bug," she said. "Is that out of your system yet?"

"It's out," he said. "I still like doing things, keeping busy, but," he said, "I no longer have that … that push. Back then that was the push to get away from everything in my life that I hated."

"Because it's easier to avoid it all," she said with a nod. "Isn't that lovely?"

"Not really," he said, "but it's nice to come to this point where I'm okay with it."

She nodded and smiled. "So tell me what the game plan is with the dog."

"Would have been easier if I'd been here months ago," he said, "but I'm not sure we'll get off ground zero because it depends on whether anything is even left to find."

"It's been a long time."

"I know. I don't understand why the commander didn't move on this lost War Dog originally, but I think somebody checked up on it, and then the War Department was closing down, and nobody followed up."

"Which is too bad because that dog's already given so

much of his life," she said. "He's a veteran, like you. It doesn't make a whole lot of sense."

"Nothing ever does, and unfortunately military animals are not given the respect that they should be."

"I know," she murmured. "So why don't we go for a drive tonight?" she asked.

"I don't know how far away it is." He brought up the address on his phone, and the two discussed the best way to get there. As soon as they finished eating, he said, "You know what? Maybe we should. You up for a drive?"

"Absolutely," she said. "Do you want to bring the dogs or not?"

He thought about it and nodded. "Yes, let's bring them. This Beowulf might have an easier time if he recognizes other dog lovers."

"Good thought," she said. They quickly cleaned up the dishes, and, as she stepped outside, she was surprised to see a truck here. "I forgot you brought in a rental."

"Yep, I did," he said. "I didn't want to be a bother. I knew I would possibly have to leave everything at the drop of a hat, and I didn't want to impact your world too much."

She shrugged. "You still didn't have to."

"Maybe not, but," he said, "I'm not taking advantage."

"You always were too honorable for that," she teased.

"Nothing wrong with being honorable," he said with a grin.

"In your world," she said, "that's like one of the biggest things to be."

"It is, indeed," he said and got in behind the wheel.

She opened up the passenger door and let all the dogs in. Not Graynor. He stayed behind.

Caleb smiled as he asked, "Do they still ride in the

front?"

"They ride where they want to ride," she said. "Front, back, wherever." She laughed. "If they're in your way, they'll go into the back seat just fine too." They quickly shuffled the dogs into the back seat, and he headed out. "How far do we've to go?" he asked.

"I've got it up on my GPS," she said.

"Good, let's go see what there is to find."

IT TOOK THEM twenty minutes, and twenty minutes through traffic he didn't think was too bad. He was delighted that her place was as close as it was because he figured he'd have to come back and forth several times. By the time they reached the rural property, he smiled and said, "Well, Beowulf should have been happy here. The property looks to be a couple acres, I guess."

"I'll bring it up," she said and quickly checked the details. "The couple don't own it at all," she said. "It's owned by a corporation out of California."

"So it was a rental property?"

"I have no idea. Looks like a shell company too," she said, digging quickly into the internet. "Still doesn't have anything to do with the dog though."

Caleb pulled into the driveway, and they hopped out, letting the dogs loose. The dogs mingled around the truck, excitedly sniffing at their heels as they walked around. Caleb walked up to the front porch and knocked on the door. She watched from the driveway, looking to see if anybody was out on the property. When no answer came at the door, he turned and looked at her.

She shrugged. "They said it was empty, and you'd have full access."

"True." He gave another quick look, shrugged, opened the front door, and stepped inside.

It was empty, as far as he could tell. And, with Laysha and her dogs running behind him to come inside too, he walked through the place, looking for any sign that anybody had been here recently. But it looked to be unoccupied for at least the last couple months. But then it was hard to tell. At least a month. Maybe that was a better take.

As they went through the house, she said, "It's just a family home. Nothing different, nothing scary, nothing surprising."

"Nope, not at all," he said. He stepped out on the back steps and took a look around. "This looks all pretty normal too."

"Have we checked all the rooms inside?" she asked, as she returned inside, heading toward the front door.

"No, I don't think so." He turned, took a second look around outside, and said, "Nothing going on out here."

"But you didn't really expect there would be, did you?"

"No, not really," he said, "but one can always hope." He tossed her a grin, catching up with her, and opened up what looked like a big storeroom door off the kitchen. As soon as he did, he backed away, coughing and hacking, holding his sleeve over his nose. She came up behind him, gasped in shock, and he quickly turned her away and moved the dogs out of the way and slammed the door shut.

"What the hell was that?" she asked.

He already had his phone in his hand. "A dead body," he said.

She stared at him in horror. "But who?"

"I don't know," he said. "I didn't want you to see that. I'm calling the police now."

"The police. Great," she said, rolling her eyes.

"Is Detective Ansel Lowery still around?"

"I think so," she said. "He'll love this." She laughed. "He bailed us out of so much trouble," she said, as Caleb made his way through several phone calls to get to Lowery.

When he identified himself, Lowery said, "Oh, my God. Where the hell are you?"

"I'm in El Paso, staying at Laysha's house," he said, "but I've been looking for a K9 on behalf of the War Dog Department," he added. "We came to the last-known residence, and we were doing a quick check because it's empty. Apparently the adoptive couple moved into town," he said. "*Buuut* ..." He paused for a long moment.

Detective Ansel Lowery asked on the other end, "But what?"

"We found a body here."

"Seriously?" he exploded. "Do you guys ever do anything but get into trouble? You've been in town what? Five minutes and you've already found a corpse?"

"It's not our fault," he said. "And remember. When we got into trouble years ago, it *was* years ago."

"Funny how the years just fall away," Lowery said with a note of humor. "I'm sending out a team and the coroner."

"Good."

"Male, female, or did you not look?"

"The dead body is inside a closed room, and the smell's pretty ripe. I didn't get a good look. However, by the decomp, I would say the person died at least several days ago."

"Well, we've had a lot of warm weather here," he said.

"Give me the address again, so I can confirm the ownership. And who did you say was living there before?"

Caleb filled in the detective on all the details, as much as he could, and said, "Laysha's sitting on the back deck. We've got her dogs here with us."

"Well, stay where you are," he said. "I'm about thirty minutes away."

"Will do." Caleb hung up and quickly called Badger and updated him.

"Seriously?" Badger said. "A dead body in the empty house?"

"Yeah. I had to pass over as much of the information as I had to the cops, but they're on their way now."

"Oh, they'll be looking for all kinds of information at this point," Badger said. "Give them anything you can of course," he added. "We need to solve this, and let's not have it derail our search for the dog."

"I guess the question is, could it be connected?"

"No way to know for sure yet, but we have to assume that there must be some connection just because it's the same property."

"Sure, but it's been a long time since the dog was here."

"Yes, it has, at least as far as we know, and the couple supposedly moved out shortly afterward. What we don't have is necessarily the truth on any of this."

"Good point," Caleb said. "I hear the sirens. I'll talk to you with an update later." And he hung up. As he turned, Laysha stood there, pointing at the front. "I know. The cops are here," he said. "Let's go talk to them."

He noted that she had leashed all three dogs, and, as they walked out to the front, two cops stood there, discussing what was going on, and then a third vehicle pulled in.

Out of that one stepped Ansel Lowery. Caleb walked over and shook his hand.

The detective smiled. "Well, it's good to see you two. Nice to know that all's well in your corner of the world, but, jeez, it'd be nice if you didn't keep calling me for the wrong reasons."

"It's been a long time since we've called you," Laysha protested. "And this is a particularly ugly reason for calling you," she admitted. "The decomp's like seriously bad."

CHAPTER 4

LAYSHA STAYED OUTSIDE and watched while the cops went inside with Caleb. He seemed to fully adapt to the presence of a dead body. And maybe that was his military experience, but, for her, that smell was shocking and then to see—which she didn't even really see anything—just a crumpled pile of clothing and something like … looked almost yellow and green and putrid. She sighed when Caleb finally came out.

He walked toward her, wrapped her in his arms, and said, "Sorry you had to see that."

"I don't even know what I did see," she said, "but it was pretty nasty."

"Yep. Anything like that is," he said with a nod.

"I gather you've seen things like that before?"

"I have," he said, "not that it ever gets any easier."

"I can't imagine," she said.

"No, it's definitely not preferable."

At that, she turned to see Detective Ansel coming toward them.

"So you want to tell me what's your side of the story?"

She sighed and quickly gave him the version of what happened as she knew it.

"Well, it certainly matches up with his. Unfortunately I don't have anything here to go on, but we'll have to run down who it is and how they got here," he said. "We've got your contact information, so we'll be in touch."

Caleb said, "I still need to look for the dog."

"Well, I don't want you back in the house," he said, "and we haven't searched the grounds yet."

"Do you mind, while we still have an hour of daylight, if we take a walk around the property?"

He frowned.

Caleb rushed to say, "If we see anything, obviously we'll let you know."

"Right," he said. "Fine, go take a look." He stopped, then added, "Actually, why don't I come with you?" And they walked around to the back of the house and headed toward the fence line.

"It hasn't been mowed in a while," Caleb said.

"I'm not sure it was ever really that well taken care of," Ansel said. "If you look closely, no grass clippings are here at all. Everything's gone to seed."

"Another good point," Caleb admitted. "So what we have is a dead body that may or may not be related to the people who were here. It's been an empty house for a couple months, so it could have been anybody's dumping site."

"How did they know about that pantry though?" she asked.

"Unless they came in, took a look, and just wanted a room to lock up the body in," he said, looking at her.

She nodded. "Still a little disturbing to think that somebody would carry around a dead body, dump them, and leave them."

"They have to leave them somewhere, and if it's an empty house …" Ansel said.

"But surely the body would be found faster than just

taking them out and deep-sixing them," she said.

"Maybe, but it's also quite possible that somebody preferred the dumping to the digging." Ansel shrugged.

"I'm thinking there might be more than one dead, and that's a little disturbing," she murmured.

"I didn't mean that so much, but it's another angle," Ansel said. "I can tell you it looks like a shot to the back of the head."

"Ah." At that, Caleb nodded. "So execution."

"It's possible, particularly given how close to the border we are."

"I don't like the sound of that at all," Laysha said.

Caleb reached out and grabbed her hand, tugging her a little closer. She went willingly enough.

"It was pretty unpleasant to look at," Ansel said. "Sorry about that."

"It's not your fault," she said, "but it still sucks."

"It does, indeed."

They did a quick trip around the property and didn't see anything obvious. As they stopped at the far corner and looked back at the house, she turned to Caleb. "Any idea on the dog?"

He shook his head. "I'll come back in the morning," he said, "and see if I can track it from the house."

"I still don't understand how you can do that," she muttered.

Detective Lowery looked at him. "You got some experience tracking?"

"I do," he said, "but a lot of weather has transpired since then," he said. "So chances of finding anything are pretty close to nil."

"Well, if you do find something, good luck. And, if you

find anything pertinent to the case, let me know."

"Will do."

And, with that, the detective headed back to the main house.

She waited until Ansel was out of earshot. "So will you tell me what's really going on?"

He looked at her in surprise.

She shook her head. "Oh no, you don't," she said. "I get it. I saw the change in your stance when you saw something. I just don't know what it was that you saw."

He smiled, looked at her, and said, "Are you sure I saw something?"

"I thought so, yes," she said. "But you're a tricky dude. So I might have misread the cues."

"Nope, you didn't," he said. "I forgot how observant you were."

"I wouldn't have said I am at all," she noted. "So what did you find?"

"I saw lots of hair as we moved about the property," he said, "but I need to look closer to see exactly what's happening here. Also a leash is hanging on the back veranda."

"So, they had a dog. Doesn't that make sense?"

"Yeah, except the leash was snapped," he said, "and it'd take a mighty strong dog to do that."

"I didn't even notice the leash," she said. "So much for being observant."

He shook his head. "It's what I do. Remember that."

"Are you happy doing it?"

"Yes," he said immediately. "It's been a good job for me."

"Good," she said, "you always were the kind who wanted to help somebody."

"Yep," he said, "and that's pretty well what I do."

"I'm glad to hear that. Are you going back into the navy? Because it hasn't escaped my notice that what you're doing currently is hardly what you were doing."

He sighed. "No, that's quite true. And it wasn't even that as much as," he said, "up until the accident, I didn't know what I wanted to do afterward. But I won't go back. I don't think I want to do the military thing."

"Can you still do that job?" she asked.

"I don't know," he said honestly. "It's something I have to look into."

"At one time," she said, "you wanted to be a police officer."

"Maybe," he said, "and maybe that's not a done deal either."

"I guess it depends on your injuries."

"I'm on my feet now," he said, "so I'm better, but I can't do a ton of physical work. And I probably wouldn't pass the physical for a cop."

"Maybe. That makes sense," she said, "but it's kind of sad."

"It is, but, considering everybody else in my unit died," he said, "I'll take what I've got."

"Oh my. I didn't know. So sorry to hear that."

Caleb shrugged.

But he also turned from her. Hiding his reaction, his emotions.

"It is what it is."

Yeah. He was like that. She switched gears. "And that's another thing about you," she said with a bright smile. "You always had that positive attitude."

"I did, but the divorce changed a lot of that for me. The

two years of our marriage, all we did was fight. I'm struggling with the idea of even seeing her."

"Is that because you still care?"

"No," he said, "not in the way you think. *Care* in the sense that I want to rescue my brother from her clutches, yes. She cheated on me, then let me think it was my baby, and that's hard to forgive."

"Got it," she said. "I just wondered if you … still loved her."

"Hell no," he said, "not in any way, shape, or form."

Laysha smiled because such conviction was in his tone that she actually believed him. "Anybody else in your life?"

"No time, no interest," he said. "I've only barely recovered from all the surgeries," he said. "Maybe, at some point in time, I'll get back into the relationship thing, but I haven't been in too much of a rush."

"Still because of her?" she asked curiously.

"To a certain extent, yes," he said. He turned, looked at her, and asked, "Why all the questions?"

"I don't know," she said in a teasing voice. "Maybe I'm checking out all the girlfriends in my head to see who'd suit."

He rolled his eyes at that. "Don't bother," he said. "I'm not gonna be set up again."

"Ah," she said with a smile. "Well, maybe it'll just be the two of us then."

"You know what? I'm damn fine with just the two of us," he said. "Because, when you think about it, in many ways, it's only ever been the two of us. Everybody else seemed to go off and do their own thing."

"So did we," she reminded him. "They just all seemed to do a better job of it."

He laughed at that. "I hate to say it, but you're quite right." He paused. "We'll go home," he said, "and I'll come back early in the morning and see what I can find."

"Good enough." As she led the way back, they detoured around the cops until they got to the vehicle. She loaded up the dogs, and, once inside, she said, "It's kind of sad that somebody lay here dead, and nobody knew, nobody cared."

"Well, the people who cared probably don't know he's dead," he said quietly. "Leave it to the police. I'm sure they can figure it out."

"Maybe," she said, "it's hard to walk away though. I want to know who he is and what he was doing here and if he had any family to mourn his death."

"Well, that's fine. We can stay in touch with the detective. He might tell us something."

"I doubt it," she said. "Just think about it. It'll be one of those cases of 'read it in the news.'"

"Maybe." He looked at her and said, "You have good skills hunting down information," he said, "just because of your job. So don't let anybody stop you from doing what you want to do."

She smiled. "I hear you."

"I'm still surprised you're at the law firm," he mentioned, as they drove back home again.

"The paycheck's decent," she said. "Not as much as if I were a lawyer. But I get to walk away at the end of the day and come home and work on the house."

"Right," he said with a smile. "I forget the house is your current love."

"Yep, likely to be my only one too," she admitted.

"Nobody in your world?"

"Nope, not since the divorce."

He gave a laugh. "We're a hell of a pair, aren't we?"

"Yep, like always," she said with a smile. "We're a great match." And she left it at that.

LAYSHA'S WORDS HAD a prophetic meaning to them because he had wondered, at one point in time, why the hell the two of them weren't together. Instead they'd both gone off in different directions. There was absolutely everything to love about her. And he figured he'd been half in love with her since he was even a teenager. But then, somehow, he got hooked up with Sarah, his ex-wife, and Laysha had hooked up with Paul. It's almost as if they were busy being busy in order to avoid what they were really feeling. He wondered if that was even true or whether that was just more made-up bullshit in his head.

One of the thoughts that did cross his mind as he drove them back to her place was that this was a hell of a time to figure it out. They just had themselves to deal with right now. No interfering family members. Sure, he would have to show up for the wedding and be good for a little while. He still couldn't believe that he came all the way across the country because Laysha had asked him to. It had nothing to do with the wedding. But maybe him coming for Laysha said an awful lot about how he felt about her.

He acknowledged these feelings again. He didn't want to before because he couldn't risk ruining this perfect friendship in his life. Instead here he was, sitting with her, wondering how to take it to the next step. And even that thought surprised him because it hadn't occurred to him, until it came up this time, what he was looking at doing. It's almost as if he'd been biding his time all these years. And here he was now, looking at how to make something of his past that he had walked away from a long time ago—when he shouldn't have.

CHAPTER 5

THE NEXT MORNING Laysha woke up and stretched, delighted to have some time off so that she could get back to work on her house. As she got up and went downstairs, the emptiness of the house made her feel funny. She walked to the spare bedroom door, which was open, and found the bed was empty. "Well, you said you would leave early this morning, but I wasn't thinking you were leaving that early," she muttered.

She hadn't even woken up when he left. That gave her an odd feeling. It was weird to think that somebody could walk around her house, and she wouldn't notice. She set about making coffee and feeding her four dogs. She made breakfast, all the time looking out the window to see if Caleb would come back anytime soon. Yet she didn't want him to feel like he had to check-in because that was too pushy and nosy and clingy.

As it was, she bustled around, talking to her dogs, cuddling them a bit, then getting ready for the day's work that she had planned to do in the upstairs guest bathroom. She was serious about getting that vanity in today, had actually hoped to have it all done before Caleb arrived but didn't quite make it.

As she lined up everything that she needed, she heard the dogs barking downstairs. She walked downstairs, expecting to see Caleb, but instead nobody was there. And the dogs weren't barking like it was a friendly visitor; instead they raced from one end of the house to the other, as if they saw somebody and then lost them. She stepped outside, the dogs with her, Caleb shouting in her head to get back inside. She walked around on the veranda but couldn't see anybody. She called the dogs back inside and said, "Come on, guys. I'm not sure what's going on, but let's go upstairs."

With her phone in her back pocket and her gloves on, she headed upstairs with her plumber tools. She managed to connect the vanity, get it settled into place, opened up the cupboard beneath, and tightened down all the piping. With that done and properly level, she caulked the back joint to keep water from flowing over the countertop against the wall and going down, and then she segregated the dogs from her workspace and started in on her tile work. She had done enough now that it was second nature to get set up.

By the time she was done with the tile backsplash that she had planned around the vanity—just behind the wall close to the toilet—she started in on the tiling of the floor. She wanted to get the whole room done, then close the door. Although it was inconvenient having Caleb share her en suite bathroom, this guest bath did need a day at least, if not two, as it set.

She frowned at that, wondering at the sense of doing this when Caleb was here. She got it done without his help. But now, for sure, when he wanted a shower, he had to use her bathroom, since he was only here a couple days.

When she finished with the last bit of tile on the floor, she was happy at how quickly it had all come together. She stood up, cleaned off the caulking on her knees, and walked downstairs to wash off. She set the rest of her tools off to the side and worked away at cleaning her hands, elbows, and arms. It didn't seem to matter what she did, she ended up covered in whatever.

By the time she was as cleaned up as she could get from washing at a sink, she grabbed a cup of old coffee, threw some ice cubes into it, and walked out onto the veranda with the dogs, giving them a pee break. It was almost two o'clock and still no sign of Caleb. She frowned at that and quickly sent him a message. When there was no answer, she got even more worried.

Hearing a sound, she walked around to the front of the house to see his truck driving toward her. She stood here with a smile on her face, sipping her iced coffee.

He hopped out and said, "Sorry. I had just taken the turnoff onto your street, and I figured it was faster to get home, than stop and answer your text."

"Not a problem," she said. "I just finished tiling the upstairs bath."

"Good for you," he said. "I was coming back to help." He stood by his rental, the door still open.

"Oh, there's more work to be done. No problem," she said with a fat grin.

"We can pick one job now and get started." He grinned back at her. "What about the upstairs bedrooms and hallway? Were you redoing all that hardwood?"

"I wanted to get it all redone," she said, nodding. "That would only leave paint and new windows upstairs."

"And what about the attic?"

"I want to install one of those drop-down stairs," she said, "but I haven't got the funds for that yet."

"Well," he said, "I might need a bite to eat first." And he leaned into the front seat and grabbed two bags of groceries.

"I was hungry and stopped and bought a bunch of groceries too. Did you get lunch yet?"

She shook her head. "No, but whatever you've got in mind, I'm signing up for quite happily."

He laughed. "As I recall, you used to be a big eater."

"I still am," she said. "I lost a lot of weight over the divorce because I felt so guilty, but I'm slowly pulling back out of that."

"I'm sorry to hear that," he said. "I think I went the opposite. I inhaled everything, but, because of my heavy fitness routine, I didn't really gain any."

"Oh, I ate a lot too," she said, "but the emotional stress was always one of those issues for me, where I lost weight. Same as when I got sick."

"I remember that."

As they walked into the kitchen, she asked, "Did you have any luck tracking the dog?"

"Nope, not a whole lot," he said, "but I did come up with a couple different avenues to keep looking."

"In what way?"

"I talked to the neighbors. They said they heard some shots the day the dog went missing."

"And they actually remember that specific day?"

"Yes, because they saw the dog tear out across the property at the same time."

"Wow." She stopped, thought about it, and said, "But the gunshot wasn't the one that killed the same guy we found in the storeroom, right? I mean, he hasn't been in that house for a couple months?"

"I don't think so," he said, "but I don't really know. The decomp was extensive though. And it is hot inside the house, being closed up and with no AC running. So the heat deteriorated the body inside, even while stopping the bigger wild animals from getting to his body because it was closed up in the house."

"That doesn't bear thinking about. What about the dog's adoptive family then?" she muttered.

"More to consider," he said. "And I'm busy updating Ansel with this new information too. Apparently nobody has contacted the neighbors yet but me." He pulled out sandwich fixings and a couple loaves of French bread.

"Wow," she said, "we used to turn that whole thing into a big sub, didn't we?"

"That's what I'm planning to do right now," he said with a big grin. And he went to it while she watched.

She put on a fresh pot of coffee, as she finished her iced coffee, and asked, "Do you think you'll ever find the dog?"

"I hope so," he said. "Titanium Corp, the company I work for now, had a dozen War Dog files. I'm on the eleventh case. Ten other guys have gone before me, and every one of the dogs was found." He said, "I would really hate to be the one guy who couldn't do the job."

She winced at that. "That would suck, wouldn't it?"

"But this one's also a far-fetched case. It's one of the reasons that they didn't deal with it right away. So they know it's a long shot."

"You're always good at those," she said with a chuckle. She picked up a knife and sliced the tomatoes he bought, the dill pickles, then the cucumbers and the onions. By the time he had loaded that French bread, it was massive. She shook her head. "I'll eat like three inches of that sucker."

He cut it in half and then took the other half and cut that in half. Pointing, he said, "That one-fourth is yours. This three-fourths is mine." And he proceeded to cut his again, so it was a little easier to pick up. She did the same with hers, and they carried their plates onto the back veranda.

"I'm so ready for this," she said. "I finished getting the vanity in place and got the backsplash done and the floor tiled," she said, "So the upstairs guest bathroom needs to dry for a day or two."

"That's okay," he said. "I had a shower this morning before I left."

She looked at him in surprise.

He shrugged. "I've always been quiet. You know that."

"I know," she said. "I was really surprised you managed to get up and leave without waking me."

"I didn't hear anything coming from your bedroom," he said. "I presumed I got away with it."

She nodded. "You did, indeed. The only disturbance all morning came from the dogs. They thought they saw somebody, but I couldn't see anybody outside."

"No vehicle sounds?"

"Nope, they barked like crazy up at the front of the house, and then they ran straight to the back of the house, and then back and forth again, as if they lost track of whoever it was."

He stared at her for a moment and slowly nodded.

She looked up at him, curious. "Why?"

"Just want to ensure that nobody followed us home last night."

She frowned immediately and asked, "Who would care?"

"The guy who shot that dead man."

"Was it a man?" she asked, her heart sinking at the thought of somebody following them here. "I couldn't tell."

"I'm pretty sure it was," he said.

"There wasn't enough to check?"

"Not from what I saw, … but you're right. We'll have to wait for the autopsy."

"Still sucks," she said. "Despite the dogs' barking, I don't think anybody was here earlier. Graynor wasn't bothered."

Caleb looked over at the big dog, who wagged his tail right then. "How often does he get up?"

"Only enough to go outside to take care of business," she said. "He's not eating much anymore either."

"That'll be a tough day," he said, "but you're giving him the best life that he can have. So there's some solace in that."

She tried to smile and nodded. As she got down to her last bite, she pulled out a piece of ham, hanging off the side of the bun. She popped her last bite in as she stood, walked to Graynor, and gave him the ham. He lapped it up, his tail thumping like a happy boy. And she quickly scrubbed his head, leaned over, giving him a kiss on the forehead, and said, "I'll still miss you, bud, but you take whatever time you need to take and enjoy whatever life is left to live," she murmured. He seemed to understand, just casually lying there, fully relaxed.

"It's really nice to see him again," he said, "and your other dogs."

"I agree," she said. "Just so many good things about having animals."

"Absolutely."

She walked back to him. "Are you really thinking somebody might have followed us?"

"No, I'm not thinking that particularly," he said. "You did have rain here last night, and I did see another set of tracks outside the entrance to the property, but they'd pulled off to the side and didn't come in."

She stared at him. "You're spooky when you do that," she muttered.

"Maybe," he said, "but better to be safe than sorry."

"Now you got me wondering who was there," she said.

"It could have been anybody," he said with a shrug. "No need to see it as a negative."

"No, but, at the same time, it's hard not to."

"I know," he said. "So what have we got going on this afternoon?"

She smiled. "If you're up for it," she said, "I would absolutely love to get those floors finished upstairs."

"Since your master was already done, and you finished tiling the guest bathroom today, that leaves the two other bedrooms and the hallway. We'd have to empty the rooms," he said.

"Which is also why I haven't done it," she said. "I figured that, while you're here, maybe we could move everything downstairs or in the garage or whatever, and then we can do those two bedrooms."

"Yeah, and you would sleep downstairs for a night or two," he said, looking around.

"Tons of room here to pile up the second-floor furniture, and we could get all of it done, hallway, bedrooms, right down to the stairs—even finish the stairs."

He walked over to look at them and said, "They'd be a lot more work, but they certainly need it."

"And a lot of new long-lasting finishes are available right now," she said, "so refinishing them would last twenty years."

"Don't know about the hardwood flooring though. I guess it depends on how much use it gets."

"True," she said cheerfully. "But you know? I still think

it's … I don't really want to get rid of the hardwood, and that means I have to work with this."

"I wouldn't get rid of the hardwood either," he said. "It's too gorgeous."

"It's also difficult in some ways," she said, "because, of course, you know there's a lot of work to taking care of them."

"But you're not afraid of work, and something like this here?" he said. "You'd want to preserve it. It's beautiful."

"Well, that's how I look at it, but not everybody does," she said with a laugh.

"I know," he said. "We're the oddities in that way, aren't we?" He poured a cup of coffee and said, "Let's go."

She was glad he was here to help, but then she stopped. "Hang on a minute. I don't want you doing any of this heavy lifting," she said, "if you're injured."

He just gave her that flat stare.

She shook her head. "No, you tell me right now what I'm supposed to watch out for. Otherwise no way in hell I'm even letting you pick up one thing." He opened his mouth, and she shook her head resolutely. "Don't even start with me," she said. "I didn't bring you here to work you to the bone or to get you reinjured." She added, "So be honest."

"I had a lot of surgeries," he said. "I've got a new knee on both legs. I've got a new hip joint. On the right there's a bone plate in my pelvis and that right hip," he said, "and I had various soft-tissue damage, and I lost a kidney." He added, "There's some muscle damage on my back and my shoulder, but I've been through some pretty intensive therapy, and I'm fine."

She frowned, as if not sure if she should believe him or not.

He looked at her, smiled, and said, "And thank you for caring, but honestly I won't overdo it."

"You'd better not," she muttered. "That'll make me really pissed."

He laughed out loud at that. "Love you too," he said. "Now can we get some work done?"

She grinned, nodded, and they started emptying one bedroom. It had very little to move, which was a good thing because then she could remove a lot of it on her own. By the time they were done with both guest bedrooms, she looked mighty pleased. "The floors aren't all that bad in here, are they?"

"Nope, but I think they still need to be done."

"Yeah, and I've got the stuff," she said, "but the refinishing machine we have to rent from town."

"Can we get a delivery on the equipment rental?"

She nodded. "We can, indeed." She quickly made the call, hung up, and said, "About an hour to get it."

"We'll have it stripped by then anyway," he said. He had the liquid stripper in his hands, with gloves on, and he was already taking off as much of the old dull finish as he could.

"It always seemed funny to do it this way," she said, "when you know that the machine will just sand everything off."

"Yeah, but the varnish gums it up, and it's much faster if we do it this way."

"I know. I did it this way last time," she said, "but there's no such thing really as *fast*. It's a process."

"And the process is fine," he said. "Let's just get at it."

By the time the equipment was here, they had the floors of the two upstairs bedrooms prepped. The rental guys brought the machine to the porch. She looked at it and asked, "Could I ask you guys to carry it inside to the top of the stairs?"

"No problem, ma'am." They quickly picked it up and carried it right to the top. Caleb laughed and said, "Then while you're on your way down, grab a load."

The delivery guys laughed and said, "Hey, good timing on you guys' part." And they picked up the final mattress set that had to come downstairs, with Caleb behind. She signed off on the paperwork, and he quickly set up one of the beds in the corner of the living room, where Laysha would sleep tonight.

And, before she knew it, they were both back upstairs, he was on his hands and knees, wiping up any residue from using the liquid floor stripper, while she set up the machine.

"I'm absolutely thrilled," she said.

"Hey, we can get a lot done," he said. "You know nothing makes me happier."

And she knew it. They were two peas in a pod that way. And very quickly, with her working on the machine and him working on his hands and knees, then switching, she knew it would take a bit, but they'd be done soon enough.

By the time she went to bed that night—in her temporary bed in the living room, waiting for her floors to dry upstairs—she was more than tired, but she was almost euphoric.

She had wanted to get that done for a long time, but often it took somebody else to come visit before you saw not only how far you had made it but also what you still needed to do. By the time she closed her eyes, she was more than grateful that Caleb had shown up. His brother's wedding was in two days. She wondered if Caleb had even let his brother know that he was here yet. The last thought in her mind was that she would check with him the next morning.

But, when she got up the next morning, once again he was long gone.

CALEB WALKED THE back of the property that was the last-known location for Beowulf. The cops had left long ago. Forensics didn't seem to care anymore, as they had done whatever they could do, and Caleb was at the back of the two acres, slowly moving from side to side, checking where the neighbor had said the dog had disappeared. Caleb caught sight of little bits and tufts of hair, and, while possibly still here after all this time, after Beowulf being missing for more than two months, it was also possible that the hair came from a coyote or any other critter that had gone through this place.

Once he found a decent clump of black fur against a bramble bush, he finally felt like he was on the right path. Emboldened by that, he went farther and farther into the brush. When he was four miles off the road, he checked his GPS on his cell for what was close by and realized a small Mexican village was up ahead. Just one of those hit-and-miss kinds of areas.

He had crossed the border.

This section of the border had no divider. Now that he was in the Mexico side of life, the dog could be anywhere. Caleb kept moving, keeping track of where he was, and sending Badger several updates as he walked. Caleb used photos to show what he found, as he kept going. When he came to the village, he stopped and smiled, grateful that he had Spanish as his native language. His last name may sound totally American, like his dad, but Caleb was proud of his mother's cultural heritage too.

At the small cantina, he asked for a glass of water and then had a cold beer. While talking to the owner, Caleb asked if the dog had been seen around here, showing him a picture of Beowulf. The owner looked at him, frowned, and then nodded. "A big dog came by here a couple weeks ago maybe. Maybe twice that now," he said with a shrug. "I don't know for sure if it is this particular dog."

"Did you ever see anybody with him?"

"Yes," he said, "but I don't know who it was."

"White man or Mexican?"

"White man." That was an immediate answer.

"But a stranger?"

He nodded. "And that also is unusual. We don't get many around here."

Caleb looked around and saw a half-dozen small houses. "He was probably heading into town."

"Most likely," the cantina owner said with a shrug. "We don't care about them here."

"I know, but you're so close to the border that it's an easy place for men to disappear from."

"They always blame the border crossings on us," he said. "But lots of people come through here, looking to get away from their own law," he said with a sneer.

"It's the dog I'm interested in," Caleb said. "It's a very well-trained animal, and I'm worried about him."

"Why? It's just a dog."

Caleb had seen that attitude more than a few times himself. "That's true," he said, "but I want it back."

"How come it took you so long then?" he asked in a challenging manner.

And Caleb got his first inkling that the guy might know more than he had let on. "Well, there's money in it," he said. "So, if you find anything out about the dog, let me know."

"What kind of money?" he asked with a raised eyebrow. "It's still just a dog."

"It is just a dog to you," he said calmly, "but it's my dog."

At that, the guy nodded slowly. "I see."

"So let me know." He opened his wallet, so the guy saw he had plenty of cash, which was a risky move in many ways, but sometimes witnesses needed to be convinced. And he carefully pulled out a Titanium Corp business card and wrote his cell phone number on the back. "There's money if the information's good."

Caleb nodded, slowly paid for his beer, got up, and walked out. As he stood outside, he wondered how long before somebody would come after him. That was the thing about cash. Absolutely no reason to give up any info if they could just take the cash from him. And the attack would come sooner than later. Particularly when he was on foot.

CHAPTER 6

NOT ONE TO waste time, Laysha quickly settled into doing the refinishing work on the now heavily sanded hardwood floors upstairs. It would take days and days of coats and coats, sanding between each, and more coats. But she hadn't gotten a coat on last night because they were so late stripping down everything. She would start fresh this morning. She kept checking her watch, wondering when Caleb would come home today, and it was a terrible thing because, with the wedding tomorrow, he needed to at least contact his brother. Just when she had finished the bedroom floor she had been working on, she sat in the hallway, ready to start the other bedroom, when her phone rang. She pulled it out. "Hey, Jackson. How are you doing?"

"Have you heard from my brother?" asked the groom-to-be.

"He's here but not right now."

"He's in town?" Jackson asked, his voice rising.

"Yes. He did arrive."

"He could have at least let me know," he said.

"I think he's of two minds as to whether he wants to show up for the wedding or not."

Jackson went quiet for a long moment. "I guess I can understand his feelings about it," he said, "but she was my girl first."

"Which is, of course, why he's struggling because he knows now full well that it was your baby that she tried to pass off as his. It's never a good idea to keep secrets."

"Yeah, don't worry. She and I have had that one out several times too," he said, but fatigue hung heavy in his voice.

"That may be, but you never broached it with your brother. So he's afraid that you guys carried on the whole time he was away on missions."

At that, Jackson paused. "Not the whole time," he admitted. "Just at the end, when it was obvious their marriage was over."

"Obvious to who?" she asked sharply. "He was overseas. Just because she decided to walk out, she still *hadn't* walked out. So you guys were cheating behind his back."

"Look. I don't want to argue with you over it," he said. "Sarah and I were meant to be together always. We had some rocky roads, and obviously there was some roadkill on the way. Unfortunately that was my brother." He added, "But I really want to make it up to him."

"And yet you're calling me," she said.

He snorted. "Of course I am. My brother's one scary dude when he gets angry."

"Yeah, he is. But still, you're the one who's trying to make good with him, so you need to buck up and apologize."

"What do I have to apologize for?"

"Oh, I don't know. I could think of a few things," she said, "like part of what you just told me."

"Damn," he said. "I was hoping to do it well before the wedding, not with the wedding on the immediate horizon."

"The rehearsal's tonight. The wedding's tomorrow," she

said. "You don't have a whole lot of time."

"He refuses to be my best man, so no way I can get him to the rehearsal dinner. Yet, if we have a big fight about this, Caleb may not even show up at my wedding."

"Do you blame him? You didn't show up at his wedding."

"He was marrying my girl."

"Yeah," she said. "The girl who was still in love with you and carrying your baby. Do you want to explain that to him? How do you think he feels, except cheated and betrayed on all levels by both of you."

"Ouch," he said. "Fine. Okay. Okay, I get it. He has reasons to be pissed off and upset, and we've cost him years of his life, et cetera, but I still want him to show up at the wedding."

"Well, then you need to call him," she said. "I made it so that he's here. Now you should probably come over and talk to him."

"But he's not even there now."

"No, but I suspect he'll be home in a little bit," she said.

"How about in an hour?"

"You can try. You could also just call and ask Caleb if he'll be here then," she said.

"I know. It's a unique idea. Talk to him directly, right?"

With that, she hung up. She had known the family forever, but Jackson was one who definitely pissed her off the most. Particularly after she realized what he and Sarah had done to Caleb. As far as Laysha was concerned, they could just keep her out of their continuing drama. Jackson had been desperate for Caleb to show up for the wedding, so she had arranged it.

And she had no problem arranging that because she did

feel like the two brothers needed to sort this out, but, at the same time, she was pretty damn sure that the brothers' feelings were not quite so easily assuaged. As for Sarah, well that was a whole different story. She had really screwed Caleb over. Just to hear that they had cheated on him also would hurt. Again, Caleb had a high level of honor about right and wrong, and his brother and Sarah obviously didn't.

No matter how much you cared about somebody, you ended one relationship before starting another. Otherwise, it was exactly that—having an affair behind his brother's back. Who the hell needed that shit? She felt sorry for Caleb because it was another blow that he didn't need or deserve.

She groaned as she thought about it and quickly sent him a text. **Heads-up. Your brother's about to call.**

Instead of responding by text, he called her. "What does he want?" he asked.

"To talk to you and make up," she said honestly.

"Will he apologize though?"

She winced. "Probably," she said. "Talk to him. Let's at least get this all out in the open and cleared up."

"I really don't want to, neither do I want to go to the damn wedding."

"I know that," she said, "but hiding from the family is never a good idea."

"Are you sure?" he said. "Sounds like a fine idea to me." And he hung up.

She groaned and sent him a text. **When're you coming home?**

I'm ten minutes away.

She smiled at that, walked downstairs, set up the coffee, then made a big pitcher of lemonade and put it in the fridge. When the truck drove up, she and her four dogs all met him at the front door. "Wow, buddy. You're off the couch. You really love Caleb, don't ya?"

Graynor wagged his tail in response.

Caleb smiled at her, bent to cuddle each of the dogs, pointing at Graynor coming to see Caleb. He took one look upstairs and asked, "Are you doing the floors?"

"Yep, got one coat on one bedroom so far."

"Good," he said. Just then his phone rang. He glared at it and said, "It's Jackson."

"Talk to him," she said, "I'll be doing the other bedroom floor." And, with that, she turned and walked upstairs, leaving him alone. She could hear him answer and figured the brothers had to work it out from there, but at least Caleb had answered. You couldn't heal anything if you didn't at least open the door.

Upstairs she focused on getting the next bedroom done, loving how that glossy look came upon the hardwood. It was truly gorgeous. Not for everybody but it made her heart happy. By the time she was done and backed out of the room, she turned and almost yelped because Caleb stood behind her, glaring at her.

"Now what?" she asked, glaring right back.

"They were fucking screwing around when I was married to her."

"Yeah, so I heard," she said, "and I'm sorry about that."

"The marriage wasn't over," he said. "Sure, we were almost to the point of separating, but we hadn't yet."

"Which is what I also explained to Jackson," she said. "Sarah was still screwing around on you, her husband, with your own brother."

"Damn right. How the hell do you trust anybody anymore after something like that?" he asked.

"I'm not sure you do," she said quietly. "It's a gamble. All of it's a gamble. So I don't know what the answer is. But, if you don't trust somebody else again, then you'll be alone for the rest of your life. And I know that's not what you want either," she said.

He shook his head. "No, of course I don't."

"So I understand that you got in the middle of something that was their problem, and they shouldn't have involved you, and that's what they should be apologizing for. She was carrying his baby, and she was pining for him the whole time, but she married you and duped you into thinking that she cared about you. And he duped you into thinking he didn't give a shit about her."

"Great, so I'm just a big dupe, is that it?" He glared at her.

"There's no sugarcoating it," she said. "It sucks all the way around. But you also weren't happily married, and you're better off away from it all."

"Yeah, you're not kidding," he said with feeling. "In the end, I could hardly even stand to be in the same room with her."

"Exactly," she said, "whereas they finally get a chance to heal whatever's going on between them, and maybe your brother will have a decent life now."

"Maybe," he said grudgingly. "Don't see how that's possible with her." He shook his head. "It still hurts."

"Yes," she said, "but not for the real reason. It's not so much that your wife cheated on you but that your brother did."

He winced at that. "No, you're right there," he said. "And yet, once I realized it wasn't even my child, I wondered if it was his, but she would never tell me the truth about the father. When she got angry, then she happily told me that the baby wasn't mine. By then, I figured it was a complete waste of time to work on the marriage because she was still seeing someone else."

"And, as you know now, it was your brother, and she went back to him," she said quietly. "And I'm not in any way condoning their behavior. I'm just saying you're in a good position to stay a long way away from them."

He looked at her, and he started to laugh. "Isn't that the truth?" he said, shaking his head. "Damn. You know what? You just have to think about it that way, and it looks so much easier."

"It's not easy though," she said. "But you know now and can move on …" And then she grinned up at him. "So why don't you go make lemonade, while I get started on this other room."

"Make lemonade? Pretty sure I saw a jug in the fridge."

"Right. Well, I figured that was your kind of lemonade, premade." She laughed at him. "Go and pour some."

"Oh, you can't be done that fast," he said.

"Maybe not, but I'll try. So get lost. Let me finish this second bedroom." She walked into the remaining guest bedroom and immediately started painting on the finish.

"It looks phenomenal," he said. "You've done so much great work here."

"And it's just a drop in the hat of my list of things to do here," she said.

"Are you doing anything else for the next five years?"

She looked up at him in surprise. "No. Not really."

"So then you're spending it doing something that will create cherished memories and will renovate this huge beautiful heritage home," he said. "So you can't really argue with that."

"I hear you." And, with a smile on her face, she got to work. By the time he came back upstairs again, she was almost done. "I figured you had to make another batch from scratch because you took so long."

"Ha," he said, but he held a plate of sandwiches.

She looked at him with longing. "That's not fair. I'm not quite done yet."

"You got five minutes," he said. He looked at the room she was finishing off and came closer to the doorway, and said, "It's pretty good timing, huh?"

"Very good timing," she said, as she sat back. "But I do want to do the hallway too."

"That makes sense. It's all ready to go, so you might as well," he said. "But you can't walk on it until the tackiness is gone."

"Which I'm hoping will be enough to let me in tonight," she said, "so I can get to my bedroom."

"If not, you'll have to climb the outer wall, using the trellises," he teased.

"You know how that'll end up," she said with a laugh.

"Yep, in a bad way." He headed back downstairs and said, "Hurry up."

And, with a smile, she got to work. It didn't take very long, as the hallway, although it was long, was a steady stroke back and forth, no turns, just those edges close to the wall. The rest went down very quickly. She got to the top of the stairs, cleaned up the edge, wishing she could do the stairs. Yet that would be that much more work, and they weren't stripped properly yet. So she slowly backed down the stairs. There she quickly washed up, smiled at him, and said, "Done."

"Okay, good. So tomorrow sand and then another coat?"

"Yep, something like that depending on the schedule." She stood and gathered the animals into the guest bedroom downstairs. "I don't want them bothering us while we eat. I'll let them outside after we're done." Caleb nodded as they headed out to the veranda. As soon as she got out there and sat down, she remembered. "Shit, I forgot the lemonade."

She got up, and a *pop* rang out. She gasped as something blasted across the side of her head, lifting her hair, and slammed into the doorframe right in front of her. She was immediately dropped to the floor, then the back door opened, and she was dragged inside. "What the hell?" she asked Caleb. "What was that?"

"Somebody just shot at us," he snapped, looking out the window from the side.

"What are you talking about?" she asked. Then it hit her. "Oh, my God. Somebody actually shot at me." Her hand went to her head. "Did they miss me?" she asked. "I don't feel anything."

"They missed," he said. "Don't worry. You'd notice if they hadn't."

"No," she said, "not really. I could be dead."

He looked at her, his face grim, and he nodded. "You could be right," he said. "That was too damn close for comfort."

CALEB COULDN'T BELIEVE what he had just seen. With her safely inside, he went from window to window, looking for whoever the shooter was. A lot of shrubs were in the back. She had five acres, and those five acres held a lot of trees, hills, vegetation of all kinds. An abundance of hiding places. He studied the area where the shot had come from. He wanted to get out and track him, but he didn't dare leave Laysha, was too damn worried that the shooter was still here.

She crawled along the floor to the guest bedroom, staying below the long windows, and confirmed that the dogs were all okay. Yes, all four lying on the floor, ears up, staring toward the back door. They knew something was up, just not what. Then neither did she. Worried, she said, "Stay safe in here, guys, please." She crouched and returned to Caleb. "Do you think he's still out there?"

"Yes," he said. "Just think about it. It's all too possible. Either he doesn't know if he took you out and thus bolted or he's just sitting there, waiting for another opportunity to take you out."

She stared at him and gulped. "I didn't do anything. Who did I piss off?"

He looked at her and frowned. "Unfortunately I don't know." He said, "You tell me."

"I don't know of anybody that I've pissed off."

"What about the lawyers you work for?"

"But they're not criminal lawyers," she said. "We do more big corporation stuff, contracts, that kind of a thing."

"Maybe. Anything that pissed off somebody?"

"I don't think so," she said quietly, slumping back onto the floor.

He looked at her. "Are you okay? Did it graze your head?"

She reached up to her hair and checked her scalp and said, "No, I don't think so. I think it's just shock."

"With damn good reason," he said. "I'm not terribly steady at the moment myself."

"That was on the scary side," she whispered. "A little too close for comfort, as they say."

"Any bullet is always too close for comfort," he whispered. "But, in this case, it's the truth."

"I don't even know what happened," she said. "I just stood up to get the lemonade. Then turned and walked toward the back door. And then the shot rang out. Only I didn't realize it was a gunshot at the time."

"So," Caleb said, "he saw us out there, and he either waited while you stood up or wasn't expecting you to stand up, and he sent off a warning shot."

"For what though? I didn't do anything."

"Maybe it was a warning to me."

"Related to the body we found," she said quietly.

"And we have to consider that too," he said.

"It's still bullshit though," she snapped.

"That it is, but it's the cards we have to deal with."

"Don't like these cards much," she grumbled.

He grinned at her. "Keep that temper up," he said. "As always, it's way better to be angry in a situation like this than to be afraid."

"I do remember some of the lessons you shared about things like that."

"Hell, I didn't even know what I was telling you back then," he said. "I sure as hell do now, after serving all those years in the navy as I did," he said. "But, until you're into these situations, it doesn't matter how much you tell people to behave or to do something, it's not the same as being under fire and experiencing that event on your own."

"It wasn't fun," she whispered. She shifted backward and said, "Even worse, our sandwiches are out there," she complained.

He let out a bark of laughter. "Well, I'll make sure that he doesn't come after them. How's that?"

"He damn well better not," she said. "I'm hungry."

"Well, just hold that thought," he said. "I want to see if he does anything."

"But you can't go out there," she warned. "It's obvious he's waiting."

"No, he might have been waiting for a bit," he said, "but I think he's gone now."

"We can't take the chance," she said, crying out urgently as he headed for the door. But he pushed the door open, and no shot was fired.

"Dammit, Caleb," she said. "You can't go out there. It's too dangerous."

"Well, I'll hardly sit here," he said, "being a prisoner."

She thought about it and then shrugged. "I can. I don't really need to go anywhere. I've got lots of work to do on this old farmhouse."

"I get that," he said gently, "but you still need food and water, and the dogs still have to go out to the bathroom."

She frowned at that. "How long do you think somebody would keep an eye on the place?"

"If they're trying to kill us?" he said. "Until the job's done."

She winced. "Nothing like mincing your words, is there?"

"I've never been about lying or making things less than they are," he said. "It's obvious we're in a spot."

"And obvious that we should call the cops," she said.

"I've already sent a message to the detective," he said.

She stared at him in surprise. "I didn't even see that."

"It doesn't matter if you did or not," he said with a gentle smile, "because it's already done."

"In that case, we might as well just sit inside and wait till they get here."

He began to chuckle. "Now if only we had the sandwiches."

She looked at the door. "What if I snuck out there and grabbed them?" she said. "We could at least sit in here and eat them."

"Hell no," he said, "if I'm not allowed to go out there, neither are you."

"Ah," she said, "but my life is less valuable than yours. So it can be forfeit." She said it in a joking manner, but, when he grabbed her and turned her around, so she faced him, he didn't see it as a joking matter at all.

"No way," he said. "Do you hear me? You're too important. I won't let anything happen to you."

She looked up, smiled, and gently stroked his cheek. "Ditto," she said. "There's a reason that we keep coming back together again," she said.

"Yeah," he said. "I wondered if you'd figured that out."

"Oh, I figured it out," she said, chuckling, "but I didn't want to be the one to bring it up. You're the one still dealing with your divorce."

"Hell no, I'm not."

"Hell yes, you are," she snapped, noting his glittering eyes. "Until you're ready to face that ex-wife of yours and your brother—and make peace or at least confront the two of them, wish them well, but call a truce on interacting with them for the next year or so—you're still dealing with shit. I'm done with people who need to deal with shit. So get your act together, and then there's time for us."

He stared at her, dragged her into his arms, and kissed

her hard.

She melted against him, completely overwhelmed in their shared passion, in a heat that fogged her brain, and then he set her back. She gave her head a shake and said, "Don't do that."

"What? Don't kiss you? Too damn bad," he said, "because I'll do it again."

"Don't scramble my brains so I can't think," she said.

He looked at her, and a huge grin slid across his face. So he pulled her closer to him and whispered, "How about I scramble your brains and just keep them that way for a while?"

"That would imply that we actually had a bedroom we could access right now and not a shooter still out there," she said against his lips.

He closed his eyes, whispered, "Great reminder."

"Just shitty timing," she said, "but I'm really glad you came back again."

"All I was waiting for, apparently, was an invitation."

"And that's just being an idiot too," she said affectionately. "It's not like we haven't had years to get to know who we are."

"And our relationship hasn't changed over all those years," he noted.

"No," she said, her tone adamant. "You just were afraid we'd changed."

He had assumed that they had changed, both of them, as they'd grown up, but what he hadn't expected was to feel the same connection he always felt with her. And holding her close in his arms, as he stared out in the direction of where the shooter had been, he realized this was the feeling he'd been looking for in his marriage. That same oneness, that same connection that he'd always had with Laysha, and yet, for some reason, had never seen this relationship as being one on a sexual or romantic level. "What the hell happened to us anyway?" he murmured. "Why didn't we see this before?"

"Because I think we were so busy trying *not* to see our attraction, so we wouldn't mess up the good friendship that we had," she said. "We were great friends, so I guess we thought we had to find someone else to date. I don't know. I only married after you married." She said, "I married so that I wasn't alone because I felt so alone when I lost you to Sarah."

He just shook his head. "So stupid. Both of us."

"Very," she said, "but, if we're not being quite so stupid right now, that's a good thing."

"I'm not planning on being stupid," he muttered. "Are you planning on being stupid?"

"I never plan on it," she said with emphasis, "but somehow we manage to do it regardless."

He chuckled. "Oh, God, that's true," he said. "I really have to face them, huh?"

"You sure do," she said, "and you'll be facing it in such a way that you know for sure that it's over and that you don't harbor any ill will because that's the only way that you'll know if you care about me."

"Nope," he said, "that's just silly. I already know I care about you."

She squeezed him tight, and he smiled, holding her even closer. "You've always cared about me but not in that way."

"I think ..." he said, "I think you're wrong. As I think about it now, I think I was always looking for that same connection that I had with you. But why the hell I didn't see that as you, I don't know."

"I never really let you see how I felt." She added, "So maybe I just hid it too well."

"I don't know. It just feels like we wasted a ton of time."

"We did, but the good news is," she said, "we're here now."

"Yep, whatever that means."

"Depends on how you feel about that marriage of yours."

"What marriage?" he teased.

She chuckled. "You're funny."

"No, you're funny."

"Nope, you're funny," she said, laughing. "And you're an idiot." She pulled away from him. "Now go get the damn sandwiches. I'm hungry."

"I will now that I hear the cops coming," he said. He leaned over, gave her a hard kiss, and said, "And you need to be prepared for lots more questions."

She groaned. "Who the hell wants cops around?"

"You were happy I called them before."

"Sure, but you know …" And she waggled her eyebrows.

"We can't even get to your bedroom," he said.

"Really, a guy like you can't figure that out?"

He stood and grinned, as the sirens blared, and the cop cars ripped down the driveway.

She looked out where the shooter probably had been. "Any sign of him?"

"No, not yet. I suspect he's long gone."

"Well, if it was me, I would have booked it immediately," she said.

"Depends on whether he thinks he got you or not." He held out his hand to help her up.

"True enough."

He led her to the front door, where they waited till the cops got out, and then he opened the door and stepped outside. The detective looked at him and said, "Seriously, a shooter?"

Caleb gave them directions on which corner of the property the shot came from, and the teams fanned out.

"What the hell did you do?" the detective asked Caleb. "It's been a long time since you were in town, but isn't it time for you to leave already?"

"Too damn bad," Laysha said in his arms. "I don't want him to leave at all."

"The two of you together? Oh, my God," Ansel said, "you guys are just bad news."

"Well, maybe he'll go into police work," she said, "and he can help you solve some of the stuff that we're forever digging up."

At that, the detective just rolled his eyes. "Like that'll happen."

"Might," she said. "Although he doesn't know about the physical."

Ansel looked over at Caleb. "He looks fit."

"I'm back from rehab after an accident in the navy," Caleb said.

Ansel's eyes lit up. "I heard you went into the military. Now you're out?"

"Yeah, sidelined by the accident."

"So what are you doing now?"

"Looking at options," he said.

"*Hmm.* Well, law enforcement might be something you want to take a look at."

"Maybe, I don't know. Worry about your physical."

"A sheriff in a nearby county is looking for a deputy," he

said.

She looked up at Caleb. "That might work."

"Maybe," Caleb said, "depends on whether I can find this dog or not."

"I still don't understand how this dog comes into play."

Caleb quickly explained about the company he worked for.

"You got any K9 training?" Ansel asked.

"I do," he said. "Why?"

"Because we're looking for a K9 unit. But I don't know that it would be full-time," he said. "So that might be an option too," he said.

"I could possibly put my services out on a private level too."

"Maybe," he said, "certainly something for you to consider."

"Oh, I'm considering lots at the moment," Caleb said, "but find the shooter, and then we can talk."

Ansel snorted at that. "I just don't understand what you got into."

"We think it might be connected to that body we found," she said quietly. "Nothing else has changed, and Caleb just arrived in town two days ago."

"So this is your third day back in town?"

He nodded. "I came after the War Dog. We had that last-known address and, knowing the place was empty, drove out to see it, that evening on my very first day here. You know the rest."

"Yep, and we checked the forwarding address you gave us, and nobody's there. The manager did say it was rented to that name though. He thought it was a couple but said he didn't see anybody move in. Yet the rent's been paid on time."

"And nobody's living there?"

"We opened up the apartment this morning, and it's never been moved into. So then it's quite possible that this does go back to that mess," he added. "Maybe you guys found something that has been perfectly hidden for a long time."

"Well, surely somebody would be renting that rural property and would have found that dead body sooner or later."

Ansel shook his head. "For a really depressed area, the rent they're asking is very high," Ansel said. "I predict it will stay empty for many months, if not years."

"I don't understand why you'd leave the body there in the first place," she said. "Surely, if you buried it out in the back, it's a better deal for everybody involved."

"Maybe," the detective said, shrugging, "but it's not always that easy."

"No, I guess not," she said. "I've never tried to dispose of a set of remains, so I wouldn't know."

"People do all kinds of crazy things," Ansel said, nodding to one of his deputies. "The bottom line is, my guys haven't found any evidence of a shooter back there. We'll take the bullet out of the wall, if you don't mind," he said, walking outside onto the rear veranda, where the shot had been fired into the house, watching forensics already digging it out.

"Do you think that will help?" Laysha asked Ansel. She and Caleb remained at the doorway.

"Well, it can't hurt," he said. "Now please stay safe and stay out of trouble." He gave a sharp look to Caleb.

As the cops turned to leave, Caleb called out, "I'm still

looking for that War Dog. So, if you hear anything about him, let me know."

"I haven't heard anything to date," he said, "but I can pass it around town."

"And, if you've got any friends on the other side of the border," he said, "the War Dog was seen over there."

"Really?" He stopped and stared.

"Yeah."

"Most of the time the border doesn't exist between us," he said, "at least on a good day. The rest of the time? … Well, that border's never going away," he said. He got into his vehicle and drove off.

"You didn't tell me about that," she said.

"No, I'm hoping for a phone call," he said, explaining about the guy whom he met at the cantina.

She stepped onto the veranda cautiously and said, "It's a weird feeling now."

"And I'm sorry about that," he said, "because the last thing I want for you to feel is paranoid in your own home."

"I'm more concerned about that asshole coming back after us," she said. "They're not chasing me away from my place, but I sure as hell wouldn't mind putting the crosshairs on that shooter."

He chuckled and said, "Come on. Let's see if we can rescue our sandwiches."

"Let me check again on my babies first." Caleb nodded and followed her to the first-floor guest bedroom, petting all four dogs and reassuring them. Also finding them all healthy. "Y'all stay here, but I'll share any leftovers with you soon, okay?" She shut the door on her dogs again.

Caleb rescued their plates and brought them inside to the kitchen table. She sat at the table and started eating, as she watched him on his cell. He put his phone down beside him and picked up a sandwich and took a big bite. They were only halfway done when his phone rang.

He looked at the number, frowned, and said, "I don't know who this is." He put it on the table, hit Speaker, and answered, "Hello."

"You're looking for a dog?"

"I am," he said.

"I know where it is."

"What's the dog look like?"

"Looks like a shepherd, all black. But big, hefty."

"Yeah? And who … where is it?"

"It's not far from here."

"Not far from where?"

"Where you were earlier today and said you'd pay money for information."

"Yeah, I'll pay money for any good information," he said, "but I don't pay money just on the off chance that the information you have is good."

"Well, what else do you want to know?" he said.

"I want to know exactly where the dog is and some added proof would be good."

"Well, I'm not going on the property," he said, "but the dog is chained up. The guy who owns him now, he's bad news."

"Okay," he said, "I appreciate you telling me about it. I need an address to meet you at."

"I don't want to tell you where I live," he said. "If anybody knows what I'm saying …"

"Not a problem," he said, "but I need the address where the dog is then." The caller hesitated and then it came out in a rush. "Good enough. Where do you want your money?"

"Leave it at the bar where you were earlier," he said.

"Anybody there who'll find out what you did and want to hunt you down?"

"I don't know," he said, and there was hesitation in his voice. "You got any other place to leave it?"

"Not safely, no. Do you want to meet?"

"No!" the guy's voice called out.

"Okay," Caleb said, "so I'll leave it at the cantina then. But I don't know if you'll get it that way though."

"Leave it for José. Put it in an envelope and leave it for José."

"Will do."

"When will you leave it?" he said.

"I'll make the trip tonight."

"Okay, I want the money tonight," he said.

"Got it. Should be at the cantina in about an hour, an hour and a half."

"Good," he said. "If you're going after that dog, you'll need some firepower. As I said, that bastard is mean." And, with that, the caller hung up.

He looked at her and said, "I don't want to leave you alone tonight, not with the shooter loose."

"Good," she said. "I didn't want to be left alone either. So I'll come with you."

He winced at that.

"Oh no," she said. "Obviously we have to do this because that dog is out there somewhere. And, if he's tied up, that's also not good for the dog. It'll make him mean."

"Well, it will take a bit for that to happen," he said, "but he's certainly not getting the care he was expected to get."

"So what're our choices?" she asked curiously.

"Well, I have to make the drop."

"You don't trust the people where you're dropping the money?"

"Hell no," he said. "And obviously this guy doesn't either. So we'll wait, be a little bit late, and, when we get there, we'll see if we can catch this guy too."

"Why would you do that?" she said.

"Because it's obvious that he needs money, and he might have a little more information than he's given us so far."

"Got it," she said. "When do we leave?"

He looked at the empty plates, back at her, and said, "How about now?"

CHAPTER 7

LAYSHA WAS DETERMINED to go with him. She was terribly uncomfortable staying at home—especially after the shooting. But it was also dangerous for Caleb to meet this guy alone. However, after finding the dead body and then being shot at, she didn't want to be separated from Caleb at all. Not to mention the fact that they still hadn't settled their future. If he was leaving in a few days, she wanted to spend as much time with him as she could. She got up, let the dogs out of the spare bedroom, gave them some food scraps. As she watched them eat, she asked, "Do we take any?"

At that, Graynor walked up to her and put his muzzle against her hand. She bent down and gave the great big dog a gentle cuddle. "You should stay here," she said. "You've worked hard all your life. You get to just relax for the last year."

"I forgot how big he is," Caleb said. "Standing up like that, he sure shows his heritage."

"I know, and he's still such a big watchdog."

"But he didn't notice the shooter," he murmured.

"How could he? The shooter was outside at the far edge of my property, and Graynor was probably sleeping in the guestroom where we locked him in. And he should be sleeping now. After I feed them all properly." She got up and quickly fed all the dogs. As she looked at the three smaller ones, she asked Caleb again, "Do you want to leave them inside or take some with us?"

"I don't know what their reaction will be to the War Dog, if we find him," he said. "It might make us appear less scary if we have them with us."

"Good enough." She looked at the four dogs, all the dog food bowls empty now, and hesitated. "Why don't we take the two smaller males? Fancy over there, the Pomeranian, has a sore foot.'"

"We'll leave her with Graynor," Caleb said. He walked over to Graynor, gave him a gentle scratch at the neck. The dog wagged his tail, looked up at him, and walked to the front door. Caleb frowned. "Graynor seems to think he should come with us."

She hesitated. "He could have the back seat," she said. "He doesn't usually want to go anywhere."

"Well, if he wants to, I'm not against him coming," he said. "When you think about it, maybe he knows something we don't."

"Well, he shouldn't be seeing any action," she said. "That would make me very unhappy."

"And yet," he said, "it's a good thing. It's what he wanted. It's what he would want. I'm not saying that we'll see any action today or that we'll see anything difficult or unpleasant. However, if he wants to come and if he thinks he should come, I believe we should let him. If he needs to go to battle one more time," he said, looking at her, "who are we to take away his last fight?"

She winced at that. "I'm not ready to lose him at all."

"You might not be," he said, "but that time frame isn't yours to decide."

"I know," she said. "It'll be deadly whenever it happens."

"Would you prefer to get up one morning and find him dead on the couch or rather have him go into one last battle and be what he is, which is a protective guard dog?" He reached out a gentle hand and squeezed her fingers. "Still, as a warrior, it's what he would want."

"He was hardly a warrior," she protested but relented when Caleb opened the door, and Graynor bounded forward. "And yet he seems like he's got so much life in him yet," she murmured.

"Lying around on the couch isn't always the best thing," he said. "Graynor's got to stay nimble, fit, and healthy."

"I know that," she murmured, "but I let him do it for so long now."

"Let's load up."

She took her three males, the two Heinz 57 mixes that she'd gotten from rescues over the years—Kali and Max—and Graynor; she left just one at home. But then Fancy had a sore foot, and it was probably better to leave her home. Although Laysha felt guilty.

They all were in Caleb's rental truck now, and he drove them down the driveway. "You don't take them everywhere, do you?"

"No," she said, as she fastened her seat belt. "I do leave them home a lot."

"It's good for them to be accustomed to both," he said in that noncommittal voice.

"Yeah," she said, "but they were also my saving grace all the years that I was working my way through the marriage and the divorce," she said. "So I'm very aware of how many emotional needs they helped me deal with."

"Good to hear," he said. "We all need someone. And,

honest to God, if that someone for you is four-legged, I think it's often the best thing."

"True," she said with a smile. "And that's something you didn't have, did you?"

"No," he said, "not at all."

Once on the road, the conversation turned back to the dog that he was looking for. "What will you do if you find Beowulf?"

"I'm not sure at this point," he said. "Contact my bosses, of course, and they'll probably contact the War Dogs Department and see what options there are."

"Poor dog," she said, "to spend years in military service and heavy training, then to be retired and seemingly kicked out of a life that he knew well and into whatever mess he arrived in here."

"Exactly," he said, "we don't know what happened here."

"Except there was gunfire, and the dog took off, and somebody saw the dog taking off."

"And, if you think about it, the dog hadn't been here long enough to know what home was."

"Which just adds to the poor dog's confusion. So now he's out on his own, either adopted by somebody else or chained by somebody else."

"It's what we're going on, yes," he said. "And obviously neither of those are ideal situations, especially if we don't know where the dog is."

"And when did this happen?"

"Not sure," he said. "I mean, there are thousands and thousands of War Dogs. For a dozen to slip through the cracks when the department shut down, that's a pretty minor percentage. But for those twelve dogs, it's not minor at all."

"And you're on the eleventh?"

"Yes," he said. "Although I understand more case files are coming."

"Why did they shut down the department?"

"Budget cuts," he said succinctly. "You know what it's like. You start with good intentions, and then the budget money dries up. So you reshuffle staff, and things get cut. And following up on more dogs that should have already been resettled becomes labor-intensive, and something nobody had money or time or manpower for."

"Makes sense," she said. She didn't like it, but it made sense. As they crossed the border into the Mexican side, she said, "How do you know you can trust this guy?"

"We're a bit early for the meeting," he said, "so I want to go and see where this other guy lives."

"But you didn't get an address from him, did you?"

"No, the tipster gave me the general area, but that's it. And he gave us a first name."

"Sure, but, even if you were to stop and ask somebody about it, you're the strange white man now," she said. Then she looked at him, smiled, and said, "Although I gather you were recuperating a lot in the sun."

"I've always had that tan leathered look," he said, "but I have spent some time in the last few months while working outdoors with the bosses, doing carpentry and just building up my manual skills again, seeing what my body was capable of."

"I'm sorry you were so badly hurt," she said quietly.

He gave her a lopsided look. "So am I. But I'm getting better, almost there. Maybe I still need to do some rehab." He flexed his hand. "This shoulder and arm have seen better days."

She nodded. "But I think that bothered you before you ever went in the navy, didn't it?"

"Yep, and then a subsequent shoulder injury just made it worse."

She nodded.

"And what about you?" he asked. "Still healthy? No major illnesses since I saw you last?"

"Nope," she said. "None. Life has been good."

He pulled up outside the cantina and looked around.

"Where are we now?"

"This is where I was asking questions and offered to pay money for the information."

"But we haven't found the place where the dog is yet."

"I know," he said. "I was just thinking I might get an actual address from someone here."

"Like, talking to them over there? A couple of young guys are outside."

"That might be a good idea," he said. They were fairly well dressed and looked like they had jobs, where a lot of the area was rural and labor-oriented. "Or they're working for this guy."

"That's possible too."

He hopped out, looked at her, and said, "Stay here, please." And he took the keys with him.

She watched as he left. "It's not like I would leave without you," she muttered. "And I sure as hell wouldn't leave you behind." Just the fact that he'd taken the keys rankled. And it shouldn't have. He had always been protective, looking after things. But that just seemed a little excessive.

In the backseat, Graynor gave a deep *woof.* She looked over, smiled at him, and said, "How are you doing, boy?"

He dropped his chin on the back of the seat with his

head toward her, and she reached over and scratched him. "I know your time is coming, but I really am not ready to let you go," she whispered. He whined in the back of his throat, and she just cuddled him close. She could feel hot tears stinging her eyes because the last thing she wanted was to go through a slow demoralizing decline of his health. But it would be just as bad and potentially way worse to put him down.

As they watched together, she saw Caleb approach the young men. He asked for a location; he spoke Spanish fluently, which was very typical of those who lived in this multicultural city. By the time he came back and hopped into the truck and turned on the engine, she said, "And?"

"Not only did they know where he lived but they also told me to stay away because he's bad news."

"Oh, good," she said, "I knew I liked them."

He chuckled. "I told them that he had a dog of mine. They just rolled their eyes at that and said he has many dogs."

"Guard dogs?"

"I think so. Whether they're up on the hills, guarding some illicit operation, I don't know," he said. "But they did warn me that he's into drugs and he's bad news."

"*Good*," she said. "Now what?"

"We'll do a drive-by so I can take a look and see just what I'm dealing with." He texted somebody on his phone; then he hit Reverse and pulled out.

"Now who are you talking to?"

"Telling my boss. Asking them to check satellite feed of the area because we want to know exactly what we're facing, before going in."

"You're thinking he's that dangerous?"

"I didn't think your house was in a terribly dangerous area," he said, "but we were still shot at."

She winced at that. "Good point. And I guess we don't want anything else to go sideways, do we?"

"No," he said, as he drove past, lifting a hand at the young guys.

"Will they remember you?"

"Oh, yes," he said. "And I suspect they're already contacting our asshole to let him know we're coming by."

"Why would they do that?"

"To stay on his good side," he said. "They're just trying to stay alive in a town where one of the bosses is a scary asshole."

"Is he likely to start shooting before he even talks to us?"

"I doubt we'll get close enough to talk to him," Caleb said shortly. "Guys like that have henchmen between him and the bullets."

"Right," she said. "Are we planning on talking to him today?"

"Not unless we get stopped."

"Great." She sat back, and they took a series of turns before they came to a very rural area and a large hacienda-looking house settled farther back on the land. "That's what I expected," he murmured. "Barbed wire roll on the top, complete with alarms and gunmen."

She whistled. "Is that really somebody walking around with a rifle over his shoulder?"

"Yeah, that's the guard on duty."

"What's he guarding? Fort Knox?"

"Probably just the boss," he said quietly. "Which means the boss has made a hell of a lot of enemies, and he's always afraid for his life."

They kept driving slowly down the road. When a bullet whistled harmlessly overhead, he nodded. "Also expected."

She stared at him in shock. "You expect to get shot at when you're driving down a road?" She wasn't even sure how the hell she could be a so calm herself because this was not normal for her.

"With guys like that? Yeah. First one is a warning shot. We get any closer, and it's no longer a warning."

"So they won't even talk to us?" she asked, twisting to look back. She saw no sign of anybody.

"Nope, not at all. That's just a warning to say, *Keep on going*."

"And are we?"

"As much as we can," he said. He tossed his phone to her and said, "Can you bring up a map on my phone? See what the GPS gives us for a route here. I'd love to circle the entire property."

"How many acres do you think he has?"

"I'd guess ten but, out here, could be forty."

"Forty would mean he could be doing something on the property, right?"

"Ten is big enough to be running all kinds of operations. He could just be running drugs. He could be manufacturing drugs. He could be moving women. We don't know."

At the word *women*, she stared at him in shock. He looked at her and said, "When you get into being a badass, they start looking at making money. Drugs are just the start of it. Women very quickly become secondary income and an equally decent income earner."

"Great," she said. "That's not what I wanted to hear."

"Maybe not," he said, "but I'd be a fool to not keep you in the loop."

"No, don't do that," she said.

"Do you have any guns at home?"

"Yeah, I got a shotgun and a .22."

He just nodded.

"And, of course, neither of those are what you want, are they?"

"No," he said, "but I can see why you have those."

"Well, I need something for coyotes and two-legged predators," she said. "Haven't really had any need for more than that."

"And I'm glad," he said, "seriously glad because it makes no sense to carry any other firepower if you won't use it."

"I thought that was something everybody wanted," she said, "bigger and better guns."

"Maybe, but bigger and better guns doesn't give you a bigger and better shooting ability."

She snorted. "I remember that too," she said, "but I haven't done any target practice in a long time."

"And that just means we need to change that when we get home again."

"Believe it or not, I did think about that after the shooting at home today."

"Good, and make sure everything is accessible."

She went silent for a long moment. "You're really expecting trouble, aren't you?"

He looked at her and gave her the gentlest of smiles and said, "It's not that I'm expecting it," he said, "but I don't want it to come and meet me unprepared."

She winced. "So are you sticking around for a while, or will I be facing, alone, whatever trouble you think is coming?"

"Well, I was thinking about sticking around," he said, "if

you're open to having a house guest."

"I already have a house guest," she said bluntly. "I just don't know what his time frame is."

"Well," he said, "believe me, that wedding and rehearsal dinner and related drama has all dropped on the radar to be much less important."

"For you, yes," she said, "but for your brother, no."

He groaned. "Back to that?"

"Yep," she said cheerfully, "it's the only way to deal with it."

"Well, I sure am glad it's a morning wedding. We'll go and leave almost immediately."

"Are you expecting trouble to follow you there?"

"Again, I'm not expecting anything," he said, "but neither do I want something like that to happen on my watch."

"Right," she said, "and I guess, as much as I hate to say it, do you think it's even safe to go now, what with the shooting?"

He gave her a lopsided grin. "Well, I'd love to say, *Hell no*, so that I can get out of it," he said, "but it probably won't get me out of anything, just cause more negative feedback."

"But, if getting them killed is part of going to the wedding," she said, "that's hardly a good idea."

"And yet think about it. Will anybody in the family actually believe me?"

"No," she said immediately, "and that's a *hell no*." She laughed.

"And is there any serious danger? I don't think so. We'll have to take great care to make sure that we're not followed, and, other than that, we'll hit the wedding and not stick around."

"That should do it," she said, thinking about it. "You

don't need to be there for very long."

"Nope, not planning on it."

"He did want you for his best man."

"Well, that won't happen, since he decided to sleep with my wife."

"Or before you married his fiancée."

He stopped and looked at her. "What?"

She looked at him in shock. "Did you not know they were engaged?"

"No," he said, staring at her, before tugging his gaze back to the road.

"Wow, she really didn't tell you much, did she?"

"No," he said, "I was away on missions. Remember?"

"Well, it sounds like you missed a lot while you were away."

"You think?" he snapped.

She looked at him and asked, "It still bothers you?"

"WHAT BOTHERS ME is that I was such a dupe," Caleb snapped. "I mean, obviously a lack of human decency bothers me that she would do what she did, that *he* did what he did. Am I hurt by it all? No. I'm angry," he said. "But I'm angry because I was so stupid. They should have kept me out of their little games."

"Agreed," she said with a wince.

"What?" he asked, suspicion in his voice.

"Okay," she said, "I'm not at all happy to hear that you're hurt emotionally by it all, after four years."

"First, some of this information is seconds old to me, and, second, I told you," he said in exasperation, "that I no longer care in any way, shape, or form."

"You can say the words," she said, "but it's your reactions that count."

"It's emotions that count," he said, "and I can tell you that I'm not feeling anything except anger toward him and her."

"But we're never angry for the reason we think we are," she said.

He glared at her. "Who are you quoting from some damn place? Really? You'll throw that New Age bullshit at me?"

At that, she burst out laughing, and he could feel his own sense of humor lighten up. It still pissed him off that his brother had been in his married life to that extent. But, as Caleb realized just how much his brother's and Sarah's lives were entwined, Caleb realized the two of them were probably better off together. At least then they couldn't go around hurting anybody else. He thought about it for a long moment as he kept driving.

She finally said, "I've got the area on the GPS, and these dirt roads just keep going around and around."

"Yeah, most of them won't even show up on GPS either," he said.

She looked at him. "What's the problem? You're looking serious."

"No," he said. "I'm just realizing how that stuff with my brother was just games to them. She went out with me to make him jealous. But, once I realized she was pregnant, I was bound and beholden to do the right thing," he said in a mocking tone, "and she probably didn't know how to get out of it at that point."

"I think you're quite right," she said. "Remember. She's

pretty damn young."

"She's only young emotionally," he said. "She's just a couple years younger than you."

When she kept staring, he looked at her in surprise. "Isn't she?"

He watched as she tilted her head, thinking about it, and then slowly nodded. "She is. Funny how I never put that together."

"That's because she's immature," he said.

"Yep, got it." She looked up at the road ahead and said, "Should be a Y up ahead. Take the right."

He followed her instructions, and they slowly went around the massive property.

"I'm not really seeing any ins or outs," she said.

"Oh, they're there," he said. "I won't be going in through the established roads anyway."

"And how are you planning on getting in, and why are you planning on going anywhere close to that place?" she asked quietly.

"Well, I have to see if the dog is there, don't I?"

She took a long slow deep breath.

He grinned. "Remember? It's what I do."

"I'm trying to forget that right now," she said.

"Well, you can try, but with me comes that kind of job."

"I got it," she said slowly.

"So good," he said. "I'm coming after this dog. If it's here, I'll be taking the dog away."

"What if it's happy there?"

"With an asshole for an owner? I don't think so. The dog has spent its time here chained up and probably beaten to make it hate humanity, so that, when it gets a chance, it'll go after whatever it was that they want it to go after."

"Do they deliberately turn these dogs into killers?"

"Sure they do," he said. "Lots of people do. They don't care about the animal itself. They just care about making sure that the animal does what they want it to do."

"Was it any better in the military?"

"Yes," he said immediately. "Lots of people don't understand, but the dogs are well-trained, and they are well looked after. They have regular vet visits, training, break times, and they also learn to bond with people, so they know who they are protecting," he said. "Guys like this bastard, they'll put Beowulf on a chain, and they'll just keep beating him, making his life miserable."

"Well, in that case," she said, "we have to rescue him."

"Yep, we sure do," he said. "Now if only I could figure out a plan to make that happen."

They kept driving for another twenty minutes. "It's a huge property," she said, amazed.

"Yeah, and I want background on who owns it too," he muttered, pulling off the road for a second. "Let me see my phone." She handed it over, and he texted Badger. Nothing quite like making legal hell happen for some of these guys.

By the time they had completely circumvented the property and headed back to the cantina, they were late for their meeting with the tipster.

"Do you think he'll wait?"

"He'll wait because he wants the money," he said. "Although we spent longer than I planned to getting back here."

CHAPTER 8

THEY PULLED UP to the cantina. "Do you want me to come in with you?" Laysha asked Caleb.

"Better if you don't," he said. "I won't know who I'm meeting, and I don't really want them to see you."

"Oh, I doubt that's an issue," she said. "I would suspect that I've already been made."

He looked around and nodded. "That's quite possible. Which makes me even less happy."

"Go in, take care of business," she said, "and then let's go home."

"On it," he said. "Make sure you keep the dogs with you."

"Will do." She sat and waited, hating as the door closed behind him because places like this could get rough. And once he was inside, he could get surrounded, and they'd beat the crap out of him, if not worse. She sat on pins and needles, until the door opened, and he stepped back out again. She slowly released her pent-up breath when he got back into the truck.

"Okay," she said. "How bad was it?"

"Nobody was there," he said. "Except for the bartender, who I talked to, but he wouldn't accept the envelope. In fact, he said, *Hell no.* Didn't know anything about it and didn't want any part of it."

"So that's good?"

"Maybe, maybe not," he said. "I'll drive around to the back to make sure nobody's sitting there and waiting."

"But surely that person would have called to let you know to come to a different drop spot, wouldn't he?"

"Maybe," he said. "Fact of the matter is, nobody called. So we're sitting here, not sure who and what to look for."

"Right." She didn't know what to say to that. But, as they sat in the parking lot, Graynor started to growl. "Well, he's not happy," she murmured, looking around. She didn't see where the danger was coming from. She studied the dog and said, "He's looking behind the cantina."

"Yeah, that's where we're going," he said.

"What are you expecting to find?"

He looked at her and said, "Honestly? A dead body."

CALEB SHOULDN'T HAVE made it quite such a shocking announcement, but, with the look on the bartender's face, and the fact that he quickly told Caleb to get out of there, Caleb realized that somebody had already blown the tipster's cover. The bartender wanted nothing to do with it. That's just the fearful grip this asshole had on this town. Caleb drove around to the back and moved slowly. A big Dumpster was here, but, other than that, he didn't see anything. He pulled up to the Dumpster, hopped out, leaving the truck running and the door open, and took a look inside. And he saw exactly what he expected to see: one dead man with a single bullet through the forehead.

He hopped back into the truck and kept on driving.

"And?"

"He's in there," he said. He pulled out his phone and made a 9-1-1 call to the local cops. Notifying them of the body. He kept his voice low and hollow, deliberately disguising it. When he was done, she looked at him in surprise. "You called it in?"

"I did on this side," he said. "You know yourself how different the rules are, depending on which side of the border you are on."

"What do you mean? No rules?" she said. "Will anybody care about him?"

"No, I don't think so," he said. "You can help this family somehow, if we find out more about him, but, in this case, obviously for him, his time's run out."

"Just because he contacted you?"

"We don't know that," he said. "I know it's easy to blame it on that, but it could easily be he was hired to phone me, and then somebody got rid of the messenger."

She sat back and thought about it. "And that would imply a trap being set."

"It would also imply that somebody just wanted to flush me out in the open so they saw who I was."

"Okay," she said, "and what do we do now?"

"What we'll do is head home in a way that nobody can track us."

"Because you really believe that we'll be followed, don't you?"

"I just don't want to lead anybody back to your place," he said. And, true to his words, she had no idea where they were, and then, all of a sudden, they were in her local neighborhood. The trip had taken twice as long, and yet she'd barely kept track of where he'd been going. "I guess it really helps to be good at geography for something like this, doesn't it?" she asked.

"Navigating skills are definitely a priority."

"And are you comfortable that we weren't followed?"

"We weren't," he said. "I've been looking since we left."

"What if they have something sophisticated, like a satellite system?"

"If that's the case, then the government on both sides of the border will really want to know about it," he said, "because they're running something pretty heavy that makes them a ton of money in there to handle something like that."

"Right, so it's really not all that possible, is it? But how can you be sure?"

"I can't be," he said, "but, to the best of my knowledge and my training, nobody has followed us home."

"Do you think they followed us at all?"

He looked at her and nodded. "They did, indeed, but we lost him in the city." He pulled into her driveway.

"What about facial recognition and all that good stuff?"

"If they've got something as sophisticated as that," he said, "I would be quite surprised. But again, we can't assume that they don't have that kind of backing behind them. It does mean we need to see if they do have something like that and just how serious a business they are trying to hide."

"Which makes an interesting consideration for the police, doesn't it?"

"It definitely does," he murmured. "Still, our problem is all about staying safe."

"I hear you." They exited his rental and headed for the front door. As they walked inside, Graynor growled. The two little dogs stayed behind Graynor. She stopped in her tracks, looked at Caleb, and whispered, "Graynor never does this."

He looked at her, around at the main floor, and murmured, "I suggest you stay here with Graynor, and I'll take a quick glance around."

"Sure," she whispered, "but, if somebody came into the house"—and then she froze—"Fancy isn't here."

He nodded, his face grim. "Stay here," he mouthed.

She reached for his arm and whispered, "Both my rifles are in the master bedroom."

"Got it," he whispered back. And he pulled a handgun from under his shirt.

She shook her head. "I didn't know you had that."

"I've brought it with me, yes with a permit," he said. "It's second nature at this point." And, with that, he disappeared before her.

CHAPTER 9

LAYSHA STAYED WHERE she was, a hand on Graynor, holding the two smaller dogs, as she watched Caleb disappear into the kitchen area. She was really worried about Fancy. She left the Pomeranian at home because of her sore foot, and she'd be horrified if anything happened to her little one.

"Please, please be okay," she whispered. She waited, not hearing much noise until she heard Caleb's footsteps race upstairs. She winced at that because, if she could hear him from the front door, then the intruder could hear him too.

"Be quick," she whispered. "And find Fancy."

Just as she was about to give up hope, she heard footsteps coming downstairs. Instinctively she stepped out of the doorway, so she wouldn't be seen. But, as Caleb came around the corner, she sighed with relief and asked, "Did you see anything?"

"No," he said. "Nothing."

She frowned. "No Fancy?"

"No," he said quietly. "No sign of her."

She immediately let the dogs in, and, to Graynor, she said, "Go find Fancy."

Graynor took off like a shot, and she and Caleb followed behind Graynor as he raced toward the guest bathroom.

Instinctively she knew where Fancy was. She crouched

down to see behind the toilet. And there Fancy was, quivering in place. As soon as she smelled Graynor's nose poking at her, she turned and raced from her hiding place, jumping all over Graynor and then Laysha. She picked up Fancy and cuddled her close. "That was scary, wasn't it?" she whispered. "I'm so sorry, sweetie." At that, she turned to look up at Caleb. "She'd only have done this if she was terrified," she said.

"Of course," he said. "That's not normal behavior for any dog."

"Just a scared one," she whispered. She gently stroked the pup, who even now quivered in her arms. "Wrong decision to leave her home," she muttered.

"I know," he said. "It also means that somebody was actually in the house. Do you have any way to tell if anything was taken?"

"I don't have a security system," she said. "It's never been necessary."

"No, I hear you," he said. "But I think, at this point in time, we have to consider that that will be a necessity coming up."

"Not if you solve this," she said. "I could go back to my much easier way of life."

"No," he said, shaking his head, "once innocence is lost, it's very hard to regain."

She thought about it and nodded quietly. "I also don't have the money for that."

"Well, we have a bunch of things to focus on at the moment," he said. "We need to get another coat down on the second floor."

She gasped. "I wonder if he disturbed the fresh coat of stain upstairs," she wailed.

He looked at her in surprise and said, "Well, the floor was dry when I was up there."

"And that's a damn good thing. I'd be pissed if somebody ruined the flooring."

"But he might have left footprints, which would be a whole different story," he said. "I'll take a closer look."

"You do that. I'm putting on coffee," she muttered.

"It's late," he reminded her.

"Yeah, but we have to put another coat on the floor," she said. "Otherwise everything is even further behind."

"I know," he said. "Do you want to sleep downstairs tonight, and then we'll do everything right up to your room?"

She winced at that. "I pretty well have to at this point."

"You do," he said, "if you want to get this done on your schedule."

"It's not even that I have a schedule anymore," she said, "but I only have so many days off."

"Right," he said, "so let's work on that premise."

She said, "I'll make coffee because we've got a couple hours to go."

"Good enough." And he disappeared upstairs.

She turned around, put on the coffee, and grabbed what she needed to get another coat on. Tomorrow was the wedding, and she hadn't even given that a thought. The fact that Caleb was still willing to go was huge, although a part of her said she should just forget about whether he was willing to or not—because they didn't need that extra stress in their life right now. But, if they could do this one small thing, then she felt they needed to do just that for the healing of the family; his family. She hadn't realized all the ins and outs of his relationship with Sarah, but obviously some things Sarah had definitely shielded Laysha from. Now that she heard his side, she didn't really want to see the witch either.

With a shake of her head, she headed upstairs. She saw him going through room by room, but he shrugged and said, "It looks clear of footprints. Must have been dry enough before he got here."

"Good," she said, "we need to buff it with the light sander."

He nodded. "I can get started in this room," he said. "I'll sand with the buffing machine. Give it a smoothing out so it'll take the next coat. I won't overdo it."

So, with him sanding, she came behind him with a very damp cloth to wipe up the dust, and then, once one room was done, she sat down and put a new layer of finish on the floor. By the time she was done in the first guest bedroom, he was in the second guest room. So she followed him again, washed off the sandpaper dust, dried the floor, and then refinished that room. The hallway was finished pretty fast. It took about two and a half hours before they were done. Then she rolled over, sat on the top stair to look behind her and said, "I wasn't thinking ahead," she said. "I didn't grab a nighty or anything or my toothbrush for the night."

"Does it matter for tonight?" he asked gently.

"No, it doesn't," she said, "and I'm too tired to think right now." She made her way down the stairs, to her temporary bed in the living room for her. She smiled up at him. "If I didn't thank you for setting this up yesterday, *thank you*," she said.

"We're both tired. We're both a little stressed," he said. "So let's get a good night's sleep and get through the wedding tomorrow."

"I hear you," she said. "For a moment there, I wondered

if we should be going."

"I've been wondering nothing but," he said. "However, I think it would be good to go and do the duty and let everybody know that we're okay."

"You mean, that you and he are okay. I don't know how you can ever be okay with your ex-wife again."

"I don't plan on being okay with her," he said. "Obviously my brother and I won't be visiting because that would involve her."

She nodded slowly. "I'm sorry about that."

"Me too," he said, "but you know what? Choices were made, and actions done, and, somewhere along the line, I'm the one left holding the bag, trying to recuperate. But thankfully I don't think that's an issue anymore."

"I'm glad to hear it," she said. She walked into the small guest half bath, wishing she could have had a shower, but the only full bathrooms were upstairs, and she couldn't walk on the newly sealed floors for several more hours. She quickly washed up, as much as she could, and then headed to the living room, where she stripped down to her T-shirt and panties and curled under the covers.

"This is like old times," he murmured from his room, the door open, and their beds lined up perfectly to see each other.

She rolled over to see him in his bed, lying on the covers, just in his boxers. "Almost," she said, "we definitely camped out enough times."

"I recall a time when your boyfriend broke up with you, and you needed somebody's shoulder to cry on," he said.

She winced at that. "Wow, that's a memory I'd like to just ignore," she said, chuckling. "You know something? We've never really looked at each other as partner material because we've spent a lot of time helping each other getting over other breakups."

"I know," he said. "I was thinking about that too."

"Still, it's all good," She stretched out and said, "It's hard to believe just how tired I am."

"A good night's sleep," he said, "will get us through the stress of tomorrow, and then we'll get back on track."

"It is midnight already," she said. "We don't have too many hours left for sleep."

"I know. Showers in the morning, the wedding and all that good stuff," he said, "but maybe by noon—twelve hours from now—it could be over."

She snorted. "Don't you wish?" That was the last thing on her mind, as she crashed.

CALEB WAITED UNTIL Laysha was asleep, and then he slipped out of bed and headed out to the backyard, where he studied the layout of the land. Graynor was at his side, always watchful, always wary. "You hear it too, don't you, buddy?"

The dog wagged his tail. "Yeah, somebody's out there. Somebody's watching. Somebody's always, always watching. The question is, why and how does this relate to anything."

Was it tied to the house where they'd been at with the dead body? Was it the War Dog? Or was it something that Laysha had done on her own that had pissed off somebody? She did work for lawyers, and, as much as she said that wasn't a dangerous job, if anybody wanted to get back at somebody, it wasn't too hard to follow them from work directly to home. And lawyers were often the ones who were targeted. Would Laysha, as a paralegal in the office, be enough for a disgruntled client? Who knew? People were ten bucks short of a load sometimes when it came to clear thinking. The bottom line was, he didn't trust that she was safe, and he was out here to make sure that she was.

Caleb, Graynor by his side, wandered the property, looking from all angles to see if he'd overlooked anything. It was a wonderful place, with a creek at the far back corner. A place to sit and just mellow out. As he stood here, looking at it, Graynor nudged Caleb's leg with his nose. Caleb frowned because, right in front of him, were bullet casings. "Good boy." After taking several photos with his phone, he carefully pocketed the physical evidence to hand off to the detective. He crouched to study the footprints around the area and noted that somebody had been here for a long time. They'd actually stalked her and sat here, waiting for either her or him to move.

Definitely a concern and he didn't know how long her stalker had been here, but these footprints were deep impressions. He thought back to when there had been any rain. There'd been a little rain a couple of nights ago but he didn't know how much. However, with the creek right beside here, it could have flooded upriver and come down here, overflowing and soaking into the ground. A little bit more tentatively he checked another spot on the creek bed, and, of course, with his weight, he sank in fairly deep.

So the stalker didn't have to be here for all that long. But, as Caleb checked further, he also noted new impressions, where the guy had knelt and propped up his rifle. Gaynor sniffed furiously but remained quiet. Frowning and hating to see such evidence, and yet knowing this was a necessary part of his job, Caleb searched for any other signs.

He found a tiny bit of plaid material, one of the red hunter plaids, caught on a branch. He quickly took a photo of it and then of the footprints, of the knee impressions, and sent them off to Badger.

Not a whole lot anybody could do at this point. But, down the road, he didn't know when this evidence might nail somebody's hide to the wall. He just wanted to make sure that somebody got nailed before that asshole came back after them. To think that somebody tried to shoot her, him, both of them, was already incredibly disconcerting. When he left the military, he thought for sure that he wouldn't deal with that issue again. He'd spent the last several years fighting a whole different war. One that he didn't really want to go through again, but he could do very few things about it if a war happened. He'd take a bullet instantly if it meant keeping her safe.

With Graynor walking quietly by his side, the two of them—old junkyard dogs—slowly moved through the property, checking out every angle, looking for any sign that anybody had been around while they were gone tonight to meet up with the tipster. He didn't see any sign of recent traffic, but, when they walked by the driveway, he saw impressions where somebody had pulled off to the side of the road. Immediately Graynor's head went down, and he diligently sniffed the area. "We'll have to set up cameras, won't we, buddy?" Caleb sent a text to Badger, to see if he could hook them up with something. Just another home improvement task to add to her list.

Graynor wagged his tail and kept on going. Caleb followed the dog, waiting to see if he came up with anything. And Caleb wasn't at all surprised when Graynor stopped at a set of tracks and howled. "You don't like the vehicle these tire marks came from, do you?" he murmured "You know what? I don't think I do either."

They were fresh and definitely suspicious. They were fairly wide as well. He frowned at that, took close-up photos, and, from farther back, took more to show the wheelbase dimensions and sent everything to Badger. Didn't necessarily have anything to do with the case at hand, but, if Caleb could trust anybody to have his back, it was Badger's group at Titanium Corp. If Caleb ran into trouble, they would be right here with him. And, sure enough, his phone rang not very long later.

"Don't you ever sleep?"

"I'd like to be asleep now," Caleb said, "but we've rattled the snake's cage, and the viper is about to strike."

"You think you had an intruder tonight?" Badger asked, referring to Caleb's earlier text.

"Yes, her smallest dog was hiding in the bathroom, quivering."

"Yeah, that's not the usual response for the dog, I presume?"

"No, we had the others with us, which was probably a good thing. This dog managed to hide. I don't know what the intruder would have done if she hadn't."

"And you think this is where our War Dog is, with these people following you and her?"

"I'm not sure what's going on," he said. "It's either connected to the War Dog or to the body we found."

"Either is bad news," he murmured.

"I know. She's asleep right now. We just finished another coat on the floor tonight," he said with a note of humor. "Nothing like coming home to doing household reno projects."

"Doesn't sound like you have a problem doing them."

"Nope. I quite enjoy it," he said. "It's very relaxing to get into hands-on work."

"I've always found that to be true," Badger said, "and it sounds like she's put a lot of work into that place."

"She has," he said. "I think as a way to ease the pain of what she was going through."

"We all have our methods," he said, "and I can relate to hers."

Caleb remembered Badger's beautiful home that he was busy updating. "I think that's the way it's been for her too. It's a gorgeous house. She's got five acres here."

"So are you coming home or staying there?"

He hesitated. "Considering it. Too early to confirm, I guess."

Badger said, "That's fine if you're staying. It's probably where you belong."

"Maybe," he said. "I don't really have a life or a means to make a living here though. Plus, it's like going back home again."

"That's not necessarily bad," Badger said. "Sometimes home is where the heart really is. We just have to find our way back again. When is the wedding?"

"Since it's technically a new day, after midnight, then the wedding is this morning," he said his voice heavy. "And, since I've been back, I found out all kinds of things that make me want to go even less."

"You do what you need to do," Badger said. "There isn't any true or not true or right or wrong way to do this. But don't just think of today and hurt feelings," he said. "Think of the long term and tomorrow."

"It's hard," he admitted. "I'm just trying to get through the day."

"Well, if you screwed up as badly as you feel they have screwed up," he said, "maybe find it in your heart to give them a little bit of distance. And if not, don't even show up," he said. "You have to decide what's important to you." And, with that, Badger hung up.

Continuing his sentry walk around the house and the property, Caleb thought about Badger's words, realizing just how very honest and true they were. And, if Caleb needed to learn something here, with his cheating brother and his ex-wife, it was to let go. However that would look like in this case, Caleb just needed to walk away from his brother and deal with whatever Caleb had to do right now. It would be whatever it would be. When he finally did another pass, and he saw nothing out of the ordinary, and Graynor appeared to be quite calm about the whole thing, Caleb looked down at the old boy and asked, "What do you think? Time to go inside?"

With that, Graynor turned and headed toward the house. Caleb loved the fact that the dog was as instinctively in tune with everything going on around him as Caleb was. He reached out a hand and gently stroked him and said, "I sure hope you can hold on a little bit longer, buddy. It's obviously been a tough go-around for her. She's not quite ready to lose you."

Graynor just looked up at him and shuffled forward.

Caleb understood that the old dog would come up to his final day, and nobody could do anything about it. Such was life for us all. At the house, he opened the door, and they stepped inside. He did a pass through the entire house, and, when he found it calm and quiet, he headed to his bed. Graynor came and laid down between the two of them and, without a care, fell asleep. Following his example, Caleb did the same.

CHAPTER 10

LAYSHA WOKE UP early and raced up the stairs, took a look at the floor, smiled, and walked carefully across to the master bath. She quickly showered and donned a robe. When she came back downstairs, Caleb's door remained open, and he was sitting up in bed, looking groggy. "Go get a shower," she said. "We have to get dressed for the wedding."

He looked at her and winced.

"I know," she said, "but, once it's done, we're outta there."

On that note, as he got up, she headed to the kitchen and put on coffee. There was something so very special about having him here. Just knowing that he could disappear after his brother's wedding was enough to break her heart, but they hadn't made time for any discussion about their relationship on a full-time basis or just how their future would look, if they even wanted a future. But how they would make that work, she didn't know; it could take time. Nothing in life was ever fast or simple. She put on the coffee and then brought out bacon and eggs, figuring they'd both do better with a full stomach before they headed into this. As she cracked eggs and scrambled them, her phone rang. She looked down to see Jackson ID'd on her phone. She answered it.

"Is he coming?"

"Yes. Did you call him?"

"Yes," he said sadly. "But there's still more to discuss. He hung up last time."

"I'm sorry to hear that."

"It's my wedding day," he said. "And it would be nice if we could avoid confrontation."

"Okay, yeah, I get it," she said calmly. "Since when were you ever so weak though?"

"Wow, you don't hold your punches, do you?"

"Why should I?" she said. "I had no idea you were screwing around with his *wife* at the end there, with him stationed overseas."

"Yes, but …" Then Jackson stopped and said, "You're right. There's no getting away from what we did," he said heavily. "All I can say is, I really love her."

"Well, you could start with that. He said he now feels like he's been a complete dupe to you, to Sarah, over everything that you've done to him. Not to mention that she was passing off your child as his, and you let her."

"Yeah, that part really got me angry too," he said.

"Did you know?"

"No," he said. "I went on a long trip abroad. That was partly why we fought. I didn't find out until I got back."

"Well, that's interesting because I'm pretty sure he thinks that you knew all about it the whole time."

"God, no," he said, "I was pretty angry with Sarah."

"And yet here you are with her again," she said in amazement.

"Yeah, but it's different."

"It's always different," she said calmly. "We are coming, but we won't be staying."

"And yet I can't do anything about this on my wedding day," he said. "I'm already an emotional wreck."

Just something in his voice had her asking in a sharp tone, "But you're showing up, right?"

"Yes," he said, and a more settled confidence was in his tone. "I am."

"Damn good thing," she said. "I don't want to be a party to you not bothering to show up on your wedding day."

"No," he said, "believe me. I've had a lot of second thoughts, but I'm showing up."

"Good, so you either call him before we get there or you talk to him when we're there."

"Well, I can't do that," he said. "You know what that'll be like, when I'm surrounded by people."

"So you might want to get it over with first."

"Shit," he said, and he hung up. He called back ten minutes later, just as she plated the scrambled eggs. "I thought you would talk to him," she said in exasperation. "I'm trying to get us out of the house."

"So am I," he snapped. "I was wondering if you could meet me a little earlier."

"Why?"

"So I could talk to him," he said.

She wondered at the sensibility of doing this now, but, if Jackson was determined to have that conversation before he got married, she wasn't sure she could do anything to stop it either. "Maybe," she said. "Will you be at the venue early?"

"I have to," he said, "but I would suggest we get there, say, ten to fifteen minutes earlier, and meet in the parking lot."

"Fine," she said, "but I'm telling him first."

"Will he show up?"

"I hope so," she said, "but I don't really know." And she didn't. She hung up her phone and turned to see Caleb, leaning against the doorjamb, looking at her. "What did he want this time?"

"He wants to see you before the wedding, ten minutes early at the parking lot."

At that, his eyebrows shortly rose. "Seriously?"

"Yeah, I guess he can't get married without saying something to you."

He just stared at her with a flat look in his eyes.

"I don't know if he's looking for forgiveness or your approval," she said, "but he's really stuck on it. He's already called me twice."

At that, his gaze flared with surprise.

She nodded. "So can we just do whatever we need to do and get past this?"

"Well, it'd be nice, wouldn't it?" he said quietly.

"Yeah, it would," she said. "Come on. Let's have breakfast, and then I guess we'll need to leave a little early."

He shook his head at the whole mess.

She smiled and said, "Just think. Nothing messes us up more than family."

He snorted at that.

"You can hardly argue with that," she said.

"I know," he said. "Just how sad is that?"

"It's pretty bad. I did want to make sure that he would show up for the wedding."

Caleb stopped his fork midair and said, "Seriously?"

"Yeah, this odd tone to his voice made me a little leery."

"Uh, yeah," he said. "I really don't want to go there if he won't even show up."

"I told him that too," she said with a half smile.

He looked at her and smiled. "You think you're pretty smart, huh?"

"Nope," she said. "Otherwise, I would have told you a long time ago how I felt about you."

He stopped and stared. "Do you want to tell me more?"

"After you married Sarah," she continued calmly, "I married Paul because I figured I'd lost you forever. I didn't figure that out beforehand though,"—she shook her head—"so it does seem like I've wasted most of my life pining for something I could never have."

He put down his fork.

She laughed, giving him a self-deprecating smile. "Not the smartest decision I've ever made."

He just stared. "I had no idea," he murmured.

"Neither did I," she said, shrugging. "That doesn't make me feel any better either."

He started to laugh.

"It is pretty funny," she said, "but not in a good way."

"Maybe not," he said, "but it does make me feel better. Because there's always been something between us, but we somehow kept it just in that friend zone."

"And I figured the friend zone was because you didn't see me that way, so, when you got married, *I knew* you didn't see me that way. I just said, *Anybody will do*, and I really feel guilty for ruining Paul's life too."

"Wow, that just conjures up the wrong image for you."

She chuckled. "Hey, it's the stupid things we do."

"Well, I didn't really see what I was doing myself," he said. "I won't say that I was in love with you back then because I don't think I was. I loved you, but it was a different kind of a thing."

"Exactly," she said. "What I didn't realize was, my feelings had grown into something different for me by the time you married. So whatever," she said. "Now we're here, and we'll go meet your brother."

"But it does make me wish we didn't have to go the route we did and waste all that time."

"Well, if it brought us where we are now," she said, "I'll take it as time well spent."

He laughed. "I can see that." He stood, and they quickly cleaned up the dishes.

Laysha said, "I'll get dressed. Be back in ten."

Caleb nodded and forced himself to get dressed as well.

True to her word, Laysha was back in ten minutes. As they walked outside, she stopped, looked at him critically, and said, "You look good."

He stopped in surprise. "Thank you. I don't dress up much."

"No, we don't have too many reasons to. I do like to see a man in a suit, but I also like to see them in jeans and without a shirt," she joked. "That's pretty damn fine too."

He burst out laughing at that, hooked an arm around her shoulders, and pulled her into a hug. She went willingly and buried her face against his neck. He held her close and whispered, "Thanks for always being there."

"You're welcome," she said, "but, after this, if we split up, I won't be doing it anymore."

He nodded, his tone grave as he said, "Let's hope it doesn't ever come to that."

She smiled, and the two of them headed out to face whatever the day would bring.

CALEB

CALEB WASN'T SURE what he was getting himself into when he pulled up to the church early. He hated all this damn drama stuff. But no doubt he had to deal with the fact that what was coming was coming, and he couldn't stop it. And did he really want to? Or was it just up to his brother to live his life the way he wanted to and damn the rest of it?

As he hopped out, Caleb turned to look at Laysha, already out of the vehicle. He realized he hadn't really even seen her until just now. He stopped and stared. "I've never seen you in a dress," he said cautiously.

She looked at him, grinned, and said, "You didn't even notice this morning."

"For that, I'm sorry," he admitted. "I was hung up on my problems."

"That's all right," she said. "Today you have good reason to be." She did a little twirl in front of him. "What do you think?"

"I think it's damn sexy," he said. She wore a bright sundress with big flowers and high heels. Her hair was up and somehow had curls on the side; he didn't know where the flowers came from, but she had them in her hair, and she looked fresh, sweet, wholesome; everything he always wanted. He shook his head. "How is it I never saw you before?"

"I don't know," she said. "I didn't notice *us* myself until it was too late."

"Damn." He reached out an elbow, and she tucked her arm through his and said, "Come on, big guy. Let's get this over with."

"My brother first," he said with a note of sadness.

"You were friends a long time before her," she said quietly. "It's your choice whether you want to stay friends after this."

He looked down at her, but he didn't even know what to think because part of him was not even sure what was coming. As he walked toward the parking lot's back entrance, his brother stepped out from the church. Dressed in a black suit, he stood nervously in front of them. He tilted his head. "Caleb. Thanks for coming," he said. "I understand it took a little persuasion, but I'm happy to see you here."

"Well, I'm here," he said. "What do you want to talk about?"

"I owe you an apology," his brother said in a surprise move.

Caleb just stood and waited.

"I didn't know about her trying to pass off my child as yours," he said. "That I would never have condoned. You know how much I've always wanted a family. She didn't tell me that we were pregnant. At the time, we had a major ripping fight because I didn't want to settle down. I wanted to travel the world a little bit," he said. "She didn't tell me she was pregnant. I didn't know until I came back, and I heard the rumors that she'd lost the baby. And that you were devastated, and so was she. But it didn't take much to do the math, and either you were screwing around on me or she had lied to you."

"Well, you know which one that was," he said in a dry tone.

"I do, and again I'm sorry. She's not the most upfront person, and she hates confrontation," he said. "So she took the easy way out, as she was petrified to be a single mom."

"And yet, you would have been there whenever you came back."

"She figured we were done for good, after the ugly fight

we had."

"So instead she threw her lot in with me and, of course, hated every minute of it."

His brother winced at that. "Well, the trouble was, she was still in love with me, and I was still in love with her. True, she should never have married you, and I can't apologize enough for that, and I'm not the one to apologize for her faults. That's her job, but I can tell you that she probably won't."

Caleb snorted at that. "Yeah, that would make more sense."

He winced. "And I owe you another apology. She told me that her marriage to you was over, and that you guys were broken up."

"Ah, you mean, when you were screwing around on me with my wife while I was stationed overseas," he said in a hard voice. But his brother faced him bravely and said, "Yes, in all fairness, I didn't check with her all that close. I was too damn happy that her marriage was over and that she was free again. I was pretty upset when I found out that she'd married you. I hated you for it for the longest time."

Caleb stared at him in surprise.

But Jackson continued, "I know it doesn't make any sense, when I'm the one who walked away, but it didn't take me long to realize what a mistake I'd made," he said. "What I'm trying to do," he said and took a slow deep breath, "is bury the hatchet and see if we can get on from here."

"I get that," Caleb said. "An awful lot of hurt remains right now. And a lot of it is directed at your wife," he said. "Or your soon-to-be wife. My ex-wife," he said. "I'm not sure how that'll work going forward."

"I know," he said. "You probably don't want anything to

do with us because of her behavior—if nothing else—but also for mine," he admitted. "We did not do well by you in any way, shape, or form, and, for that, I'm really sorry."

Caleb stared at his brother in surprise. Of all the things he'd expected, this was not it. It also showed a ton of maturity coming from his kid brother, who found it easier to walk away from any strife. In that regard, Jackson and Sarah were the same. "Where do you see us going from here?" Caleb asked Jackson.

"I want what I always wanted. I want you to stand up as my best man," he said. "But I will understand if you refuse because of Sarah. And I also understand that, from here on, you probably won't want to spend any time with us because of her. Yet I will tell you that she's pregnant again and that you're about to become an uncle."

That shock wave just hit him like a ton of bricks too. Caleb and Sarah had always talked about having kids and raising them together.

"I know that'll bring up a lot of other emotions and hard feelings," Jackson said. "I don't know how to make it right, so if you've got any suggestions, please let me know." And, with that, he fell silent. He just stared at Caleb, not knowing what to say. Jackson turned toward Laysha.

CHAPTER 11

IF THEY COULD just get out of this without an explosion, Laysha would be happy. By the time the wedding ceremony was over, she saw that Caleb, although still stiff, had warmed up slightly to his brother—yet held himself apart, not being, in any way, agreeable to Sarah. As the paperwork was finished, Caleb stood and stiffly shook hands with both of them, which was probably as much as he was capable of doing right now, and immediately looked at Laysha with a head nod toward the door. She bounded to her feet, congratulated the couple, giving them both a hug, and then said, "As promised, we have to leave."

Jackson beamed. "Thank you."

Caleb nodded and said, "Take care of yourself." And he half dragged Laysha out the doorway. As soon as she got outside, she said, "Well, you almost made it through the whole event without being ignorant."

He snorted. "Hell, I deserve a medal. I wanted to smack her to the ground."

"But you didn't, and I'm really proud of you."

He looked at her, grinned, and said, "I did good, didn't I?"

She laughed. "And that sounds like a two-year-old," she said, "but yes. You did good."

He motioned at the truck. "Come on. Let's go."

"Where are we going?"

"Well, we can either finish your floors or we can get back on the trail of the dog."

"Regardless we have to change clothes. If we're driving to find Beowulf," she said, "I want to bring all my dogs with me."

He considered that and then said, "Well, why don't we go home, put another coat on the floor—if it's ready. It's not been twenty-four hours yet, so we'll have to check it. Then we'll take everybody on a road trip."

"That works for me," she said.

As soon as he pulled out of the parking lot, she looked back to see the married couple, standing on the front steps of the church, talking with a few of the other guests, their arms wrapped around each other.

"At least they look happy," she said. She thought back to the stunned look on Sarah's face when she'd seen her first husband standing at the altar. "I don't think Sarah thought you would show up."

"I'm sure she didn't," he said. "But, whether I like it or not, she's family again."

"Not to mention you will be in her wedding photos." With that, Laysha reached over, patted his knee, and said, "She is family, indeed. However, remember that family is what you're born into, but friends are the ones you choose."

He laughed, grabbed her fingers with his free hand, and held them flat on his thigh. "Well, I know one friend I choose."

"That's the thing," she said in the meditative voice. "We've always been able to talk, always been able to communicate."

"Yet you never once told me that you wanted to spend

any private time with me," he said, shooting her a look.

"Didn't know it myself," she quipped. "Neither did you for me."

"No, and I'm still trying to figure out why the hell we missed all those cues," he murmured.

"Most likely," she said, "because we were so busy living life in every other way."

"Maybe," he murmured. As they drove back home again, almost halfway there, he asked, "Where to from here then?"

"Well, let's first solve whatever shooter issue we've got going on," she said. "And it'd be nice to get the damn floors done upstairs so I can get back into my bedroom."

He snickered at that. "Hey, you're the one who started this project."

"Don't remind me," she said. "There's never a good time to refinish floors while you currently live in the place."

"No. Usually the best time is before you move in," he said.

"Well, that didn't happen," she said, "so this was second best."

"You mean, waiting till I showed up," he said drily.

"Absolutely. Then I didn't have to do it all alone," she said with a cheeky grin.

He laughed. "Tell me what other plans you have for the place."

She filled him in on the gist of it, knowing that some of the plans would take years to get off the ground, and, maybe by then, she wouldn't care about them, but it was fun to talk about. "What about you?" she asked. "Have you thought about buying a place?"

"No, I haven't," he said. "That whole recovery thing sidelined me for future plans, and, when I did see that I was slowly regaining my normal health, I wasn't sure what to do in any aspect. Still not in some ways. I don't have a job. Not exactly sure what to do about a career."

"Well, you do have a job," she said gently. "It might not be a career job right now, but it is something."

He looked over at her and frowned.

She said, "Beowulf."

"Well, there's no payment for that," he admitted. "It's purely voluntary."

"And I love that even more," she said warmly.

He shook his head. "Only you would. Most people think it's a waste of my time."

"Hell no," she said forcibly. "Those dogs deserve everything we can give them. If that means freeing them from an ugly situation and giving them a better one, then that's what should be done."

"See? I knew I liked you."

She burst out laughing. As they drove up the long driveway to her place, she looked around. "How would we ever tell if there was a visitor?" she asked.

"If they are any good, it's pretty hard," he said. "Honestly, if you don't have any security system and motion sensors and video tracking, I don't know how you would. Particularly when there are no tracks to show any new presence around."

"That's what I was afraid of," she said, "but I'm not sure what I'm supposed to do about it."

"We'll solve the problem," he said.

"Once you find the dog, you're leaving though, aren't you?"

He looked at her in surprise and then shrugged. "Are you sending me away? I thought we were past that."

"And I thought you had to go home, and we would see how the long-distance thing worked."

"Hell with that," he said. "I have no intention of doing a long-distance relationship."

"So," she asked, "have you made any plans yet?"

"Sure haven't," he said with a big cheeky grin. "But you could probably talk me into anything."

She smiled, and, as they pulled up outside the house, he shut off the truck, and they could hear the dogs all inside. "You should put a front fence around here," he said, "and a doggy door, so they at least can come out to the front yard when they want to."

"It's on the list," she said, as she hopped out. She looked down at her dress and said, "At least I got to wear this for a couple hours."

"Yeah," he said. "I can't wait to get out of this monkey suit."

"Well, we're not refinishing floors in these outfits," she murmured.

"Nope, we aren't, but, at the same time," he said, "I'm just glad to have that behind me." As he walked up the front steps, his phone buzzed. He looked down and laughed. "My boss just asked if I made it through the wedding."

"Tell him you did and with flying colors," she said with a smile. She walked in and greeted the dogs, trying to keep them from jumping up on her dress, but, as soon as one did, it seemed they all threw out their good manners and jumped. Eventually she got free, and she kicked off her heels, raced upstairs, checking out the floor. She went down the hallway on her bare feet. It looked pretty decent but felt a little tacky in some spots. She quickly changed into her jeans and a T-shirt and, putting socks on, she walked back across the floor.

As she came downstairs, he came out of his bedroom. "The floors aren't done," she murmured.

He nodded.

"We need to give it another six or so hours. Sounds like road-trip time to me."

"I'm good with that," he said. "Let's see what you've got in the fridge. We have to do some grocery shopping at some point."

She checked out the fridge and realized it would be sandwiches again. But that was okay because she loved sandwiches. By the time she had them made, he had the dogs fed and coffee made. They sat down with their sandwiches and a cup of coffee, and she asked, "Do you have a game plan for the dog?"

"Yep," he said.

"Oh, what's that?"

"I'll tell you later."

Not long afterward, they quickly got ready to go, all the dogs in tow—this time not leaving Fancy behind—as they headed out toward his big rental truck.

"What are you doing?" she asked, as he did something to her front door.

"I set it up to see if anybody goes in while we're gone," he said quietly.

She stared at him, looked back at the door. "And how did you do that?"

"Setting a hair in the doorjamb, and, when somebody opens the door, the hair falls. It's basically hard for them to see at the time, but it's easy for me to see if it's still there when I get back."

"Did you do it on the back door too?"

"I did," he said, "when you went to the bathroom, before leaving."

"Wow," she murmured, "I didn't know."

"And that makes it a nice and easy thing to do," he said.

She nodded, and they loaded up in his truck and headed out toward the area where the asshole's property was. "Are we going back inside that empty house?" she asked nervously.

"No," he said. "However, I want to go back up and around from this side to see just how far the dead-body house is from the asshole's property."

"The drug dealer?"

"If that's what he is, yes," he said.

"Are we walking it?"

"That was the plan," he said. He looked down at her footwear and nodded. "Those are okay to walk in, aren't they?"

She stared at her hiking boots. "Yeah," she said. "I wasn't exactly sure where and what we were doing."

"Good thinking," he said.

"No," she said. "I was just more or less grabbing at straws to figure it out."

"Well, rough terrain tends to be the name of the game here," he said, "so we'll see." He pulled into the property where the body had been, and he saw no sign of police activity or that anybody had been here recently.

"Do you need to go back inside?" she asked, as she got out with all the dogs milling around her feet.

"No, I don't think so," he said. "I'm not sure if that dead body has anything to do with my War Dog or not, but, at the moment, I want to take a walk toward the asshole's property."

"Is it close?"

He looked at her with a smile and said, "Very."

She stared at him in surprise. "Oh, wow," and then she turned to look at the hills. "It's just the other side of there, isn't it?"

"Yes, but, because so much of this land is undeveloped acreage, we don't have easy access."

"So this rental property could have been involved in whatever is going on at that property where your War Dog may be," she said, slowly figuring out how all this might be connected.

"Well, that's one theory I'm operating on."

"I like it," she said, "and it's sensible."

"Well, I don't know how sensible," he said, "but it's certainly doable, given the locations are roughly adjacent."

"Perfect," she said, and they headed out behind the house. She turned to look back and said, "It's creepy."

"It is," he murmured. "And we might have to go there afterward." He glanced at her. "But I don't want to upset you."

"I'm stronger material than that," she said quietly. "If that'll help solve this, then that's what we need to do."

He grinned, reached out a hand, and snagged hers in his. "I like somebody who's up for a challenge," he murmured.

She snorted. "Hell, you just want free rein for the challenge," she said with a smile.

"I do," he said.

"Besides, it's a beautiful day," she murmured.

"It is, indeed, and all of that is very important."

"It is."

They walked in peace and quiet, just the dry ground and debris crunching underneath their feet. Mostly this land was a lot of dirt, rocks, and a little bit of underbrush, not a whole lot of anything else.

"It's been dry for a while," she said, looking around. "I'm surprised we don't get more fires here, but I guess there's not a whole lot to burn."

"Nope, there isn't," he said, as he looked around, noting how little brush was out here.

"You don't think of it as this dry and deserted here."

"Well, this pocket is obviously one of the worst areas," he said. "Or it's been deliberately cleared."

"Why would somebody do that?" she asked.

He looked at her slowly. "Better visibility."

She stopped in her tracks. "You think we're being watched?"

"It's always been a possibility," he said, "and one of the reasons I wanted to come in this direction."

"Why is that?" she asked, looking around nervously.

"Just in case they had better access than I thought out here," he said. "Whether it's boots on the ground or birds in the air."

"Are we likely to get shot at again?"

"I sure hope not," he said, "but it is a possibility."

"Do you think they have a lookout atop that hill?" she asked.

"Why don't we head into the trees and stay as clear of the open land as we can," he said. "Then we'll have a better idea."

She followed his lead, fear choking her throat. "I wouldn't be terribly happy if we got shot," she muttered.

"I wouldn't be happy at all if we got shot," he said. "Never fear. I wouldn't have brought you here if I thought that was a high possibility of occurring."

"And why do you say that?"

"I checked the topographical maps Badger sent me," he said, "and the bad guys are down on the other side of the hill, not at the top of the hill."

"Ah, so they can't see us approaching. Got it." And she picked up her pace.

CALEB GLANCED AT Laysha, marching strong at his side. She wasn't one to complain and had always been somebody who could keep up. He still didn't understand how he never saw her as a potential partner, when they'd spent so much time together. Maybe it was a case of too much time where they hadn't seen the possible benefits, not looking beyond the great friendship they had. He didn't know.

At the same time, he had had other things to focus on: his divorce, his injury, his rehab. This morning he'd survived his brother's wedding, and, although that had been a pain in the ass, it was over, and he could move on now. He wished his brother well, but Caleb had his own doubts that anybody who could play the games that Sarah did would have Jackson's best interests at heart.

But Caleb knew for a fact that Laysha wouldn't tolerate this negative thinking, so he was prepared to put it aside. Besides, it was his brother's choice, not Caleb's. He had already made his own damn mistakes, and he didn't want to repeat any of those again either. He marched steadily beside her, enjoying just being out in the fresh air, the dogs moving quietly at their sides, enjoying the freedom found in Mother Nature. "Do you get the dogs out much?"

"All the time at home," she said. "We like to traipse the five acres regularly. It just makes me happy to know that it's mine."

"With good reason," he said with feeling.

"Another ten-acre piece is beside me," she said enviously. "No house or anything is on it, and I can't afford it, but it would be nice to add that to the portfolio."

"What would you do with another ten acres?"

She laughed. "No clue," she said, "but, since I can't afford it, it's really not an issue."

"Well, it is kind of," he said, "just because you are always trying to expand. Do you see a purpose behind it, or is it you just want more space between you and the world?"

"Well, I think more space between me and the world is part of it," she said, "and I just like to know that nobody can be there beside me. No condo, no suburban development, no nothing will go up there."

"God, that would be awful," he said, staring at her. "Is there any talk about it?"

"You know what a new development is like," she said. "It comes in before you've had a chance to even do much in the way of arguing. They've already got all their permits and plans down, and it's just going through the motions to see if any of the neighbors complain."

"Have you met any of your neighbors?"

"Not really," she said, "not many, and I don't know their names. We smile in passing, but that's about it. I honestly think that's the way everybody there likes it."

He smiled. "They're all there for the same reason you are," he said. "Peace and quiet."

"Who can blame them?" she said. "We go to work, come home from a pretty crazy world out there. I'm dealing with all the headaches but need the job to get that paycheck, so I can go back home again and rehab my house."

He laughed. "But having your own five acres and the peace and quiet make it all worthwhile, doesn't it?"

"Yep," she said. "Wouldn't have it any other way." She looked at him. "What kind of work were you doing for your boss?"

"Everything from security to building porches," he said with a smile. "There's a whole group of us. Titanium Corp is employing veterans coming out of rehab, so—depending on our health, physical abilities, strength, things like that—we're all involved to a certain extent in all avenues. They have some guys doing more security because that's what they like, and some of us would rather swing a hammer than do security," he said, "but we all pitch in wherever we need to."

"So are they builders, like constructing developments and stuff?"

"No, not yet, although I think there's talk of it. Just not sure they're all that gung-ho about it at this point."

"You have to be pretty dedicated to want to," she said.

"At the moment, they're still all trying to make sure that everybody at the original level of bosses have homes," he said. "They're quite a crew."

He proceeded to tell her some of Badger's and his team's story. She hung on every word, and he loved that about her. He didn't know if she was truly interested, but it seemed like she was. By the time he fell silent, she was too. "That's amazing," she murmured. "And how very sad to think of a betrayal at that level."

"Betrayal at any level is sad," he said. "Just let me tell you about it."

She winced. "Yeah, my wording wasn't the best, was it?"

"But you don't have to watch your wording with me," he said. "That's the good thing about us."

She smiled. "Now that Jackson's wedding is over, how do you feel about the whole mess?"

"Better for sure," he said. "Still a little confused and, yes, I'll admit a little angry, but I think still more so at my brother's behavior than at hers."

"Why is that?"

"I think because, in some ways, I expected it from her, after seeing how much she cheated on me, lied about the baby being mine—hell, how she married me to make Jackson jealous."

"Ouch," she said. "And I guess that's to be expected too. Once you hear her lies, it's hard to believe anything she says anymore, isn't it?"

"Absolutely." He smiled, looked at her, and asked, "What about you?"

"What about me?"

"How did you feel the wedding went?"

"I'm glad it wasn't a bigger drama. I'm glad they didn't make a bigger deal out of it. There's been enough hard feelings over their relationship," she said, "and it feels good that it's done with. They're off in their own little happily married world now, and they can play their own mixed-up games, and they can leave the rest of us alone."

He burst out laughing. "Oh, my God," he said, "that's perfect."

She smiled up at him. "Well, it's true," she said. "There's been a lot of hurt feelings and upsets that none of us needed. So it's nice to have the wedding over and done with, and we don't have to see them again."

"Deal," he said. "At least not until we're ready."

"Agreed."

As they approached the hill, he held a hand up and said,

"I'll go up alone, just so I can check it out first. You and the dogs stay here," he warned.

She sat down immediately on a big rock. "Go for it," she said. "I'm not hero material."

"Ha," Caleb said, "you're more heroic than most people."

And, with that, he headed up the hill. As soon as he crested the top, he crawled along the ground until he was at the edge, where he studied the other side. This really was a peak rising up between the two properties. And that often made people feel secure, but it should have made them wary. It was pretty easy to approach from this side and have them down there unaware of exactly what was happening. Caleb saw sanctuaries down below, and people were outside at the back of the main house. In fact, some argument appeared to be going on, but it was too far away for Caleb to hear or to see clearly.

Wishing he had brought binoculars along, he studied the area and sent Badger several messages. It looked like this could be easily connected to the murder at the rental house because all they had to do was carry the body to the property, and nobody would have known or seen anything. Surely the cops would have taken a closer look at the surrounding properties, but then Caleb didn't know for sure about that.

However, would anyone consider carrying a dead body that far? Especially on rough terrain with a hill involved? But maybe somebody was on a dirt bike or a 4x4 or something, even a horse. They could easily carry the body from house to house that way.

Caleb didn't know if the man had been killed first or if he'd been taken into the house and shot there. If he'd come willingly, it's quite possible that he'd been sent and, at the same time, had been taken out by somebody he didn't even know.

Caleb used his phone to take as many pictures as he could, even though he was a long way off, and he could only zoom in so close. He could download them later to his laptop and then zoom in closer. Realizing that nobody even looked in his direction or seemed to be aware of what was going on atop this hill, Caleb studied the layout, calculating how close he could get to the compound.

As he studied the far-left side of the property, he saw kennels and dogs chained up, all lying around, mingling, completely unconcerned about his presence. Then the dogs weren't thinking that this hill was within their range of space to guard. Yet, when Caleb did climb down this hill, he was pretty sure the dogs would kick up a ruckus. He needed enough time to reach them, to look them over, and to locate the one he came to find.

If the other dogs were badly treated, he'd take them all too. But it was hard to know from this distance. Just as he turned to watch the humans again, two men stood in front of somebody seated, and then a shot rang out. The guy in the middle fell back. Even Caleb, from where he sat, could see that the man was dead.

CHAPTER 12

LAYSHA HEARD THE shot and turned to look up the hill. She couldn't see any sign of Caleb, and, with her heart in her throat, she wondered if he'd been shot. But he quickly scrambled down toward her, his face grim. She stared at him. "What was that all about?" she said, keeping the dogs close.

"A whole complex is down there. In the back of the main house, three men stood, until one was seated and was shot dead," he explained. Suddenly he grabbed her arm and said, "Let's go."

"Were you seen?"

"I don't know," he said, "but he's just murdered somebody else, so anything that makes noise right now will make him suspicious."

"Are you sure it's a him?"

He turned and said thoughtfully, "No, I'm not. I'm just assuming it was the same asshole we've been warned about."

"What about the dogs?"

"I did see four off to the side," he said. "One separated, and that might be the one I'm looking for."

"We have to get it out of there before he shoots them."

"I suspect he does that regularly, if they aren't mean enough."

"Great," she said. "What about right now? While everybody is more concerned about the murder?"

"Maybe," he said, "but not with you and the dogs here."

"Well," she said, "why don't I leave you here, and you can go do your thing. I don't know if you want to get close enough or if you need backup," she said worriedly. "I don't want to send you into anything that's dangerous, but it seems like maybe, if the asshole's really focused on dealing with the fallout from his recent actions, that maybe this is a good time."

Caleb pondered that for a moment, looked at her, gave her a big kiss, and said, "You know what? You're very bright."

"No, it's feeling like a stupid idea," she said in alarm. "Forget I said anything."

"No," he said, "you're right." He pulled out a Titanium Corp card and wrote down an address on the back and said, "Take the truck and the dogs and drive here."

"Where is that?"

"It's the cantina," he said. "Even though I know you don't know where it is, your GPS should tell you. I'll meet you there." He stopped and thought about it and said, "Make it two hours from now."

"And if you're not there?" she asked, frowning, hating the idea of leaving him.

"I'll contact you if I'm late."

"And I'm not supposed to phone you, I suppose?"

"No, don't," he said. "I'll have it off, and, if I don't have it off, you'll give away my position."

"Shit," she said. "I really don't want you doing this."

"Maybe not," he said, "but I still think it's a better idea now than later."

"Yeah, but it was my idea, so I get to rescind it and to tell you to forget about it."

"No, I was thinking about it on the way down the hill," he said, "figuring out just what that shot would mean."

"Well, it means he's got to deal with a body now," she said, "but I don't know what that'll entail."

"Exactly," he stopped and said, "and I need to go."

She gave in, knowing there was no point arguing further. "Go," she said, "but please don't get yourself shot."

He gave her a big fat grin and said, "I won't." And he turned and disappeared.

She stayed and watched him for a long moment, and then, her feet lagging, she headed toward the truck. She had to do as he'd said. And generally he was a man for the job, but, in this case, she hated the fact that he'd actually seen a guy killed. It just made it all that much worse. It also put the dogs in that kennel in more danger, although she didn't know why because surely the dogs were a separate issue.

But, if that asshole was in that kind of a mood where he was pissy and didn't like something, it was pretty easy to pull the trigger a second and then a third time. And maybe, just maybe, Caleb had an instinct in this that she didn't. With the dogs dragging their feet now, not liking that Caleb had taken off without them, she urged them along with her, as she made her way back to the empty house.

Even just looking at that house made her cringe. And was the dog stolen from there? Maybe gunshots were so commonplace down the hill that the dog broke his leash and ran to help, due to the dog's extensive military training. Maybe it had been taken from here or had run away, and it ended up in a way worse place. And maybe the dog was a completely separate issue.

She rushed the last few yards to Caleb's truck, making sure all the dogs were inside, then hopped in, and turned it on. Laysha headed out of the driveway, putting as many miles between her and that damn house as she could. It was just plain creepy to think that somebody had been murdered and left in there. Then she thought about somebody being murdered ten minutes ago, and she grew quiet and sad. "It's an ugly world out there," she said to Fancy, who was cuddled up against her. Fancy whimpered a little bit, and Laysha reached a hand down and just cuddled her. "We'll be okay," she said.

She wasn't sure how this nightmare had gotten into her life and what she was supposed to do about it. But it was what it was, and right now all she was concerned about was getting Caleb back to her. Safe and sound and in one piece preferably. As she drove, she followed her GPS's instructions, trying to find the cantina, realizing just how big the countryside was out here and how few crossroads there were.

If she could have traveled as the crow flew, it would have been fine. She didn't know if her navigation skills were up to something like that. Besides, Caleb had said *two hours*, and, at this rate, she would need all of that time. She hated even thinking about waiting on the other end for him to never come. And yet the thought just wouldn't leave her alone.

She drove until she found the cantina again. Passing it once, she went to a small shop, walked inside, and picked up a few necessities that she liked to keep on hand. Besides, they were selling coffee too. She pulled out some money, paid for the groceries and the coffee, and hopped back into the truck. Then she drove in the direction of the cantina and pulled into its large parking lot with a bunch of vehicles. She waited for Caleb's two-hour time frame to expire. The last thing she wanted to do was go to the cantina and sit there and look suspicious.

CALEB

Even on this property, the adjacent parking lot, she looked suspicious because she hadn't gotten out of her vehicle. She drove forward and around town, knowing that anybody watching her would keep track of these movements too. Also not a good deal. By the time the two hours were up, she was parked outside the cantina again. She wondered if she should go in but did not want to. A single white woman wasn't happily welcomed here. And, if they were, it was for all the wrong reasons.

That thought had her remembering what else this bad guy might have been into. *Women.* And that was scary too. She also remembered how Caleb found his tipster dead in the Dumpster in the back alley of this property, and that was nothing she wanted to get close to either. She worried about his instructions. She knew she was here to pick him up, but what if he didn't show? What if he didn't call to reschedule the time for pickup? Was she supposed to leave—without him—at the end of the two hours?

"What the hell?" she muttered out loud. "What have you got me into?" she murmured.

CALEB SNUCK ALONG the backside of the hill, coming down behind the ridge, until he could walk all the way around there. He stopped in the cover of a copse and studied the dogs. He was close to one of the big dog shelters, and all the dogs were chained up. Most of them looked to be pissed or angry, some of them quite likely well past rehabilitation. But he didn't know that for sure. He studied the one separated off to the side, who was lying down, looking forlorn, possibly even injured. He called out softly, "Beowulf?"

The dog's ears twitched, and slowly he lifted his head and looked behind him. And Caleb gave a very light whistle that he would have used in the military. The dog immediately struggled to his feet, and he realized the dog had one injured back leg. From what, Caleb didn't know. But that's why Beowulf was separated from the pack like that. The other dogs would have attacked him and taken him out.

Only the strongest would survive, particularly if they had been trained that way.

The dog limped as close as he could and then stopped because he was chained up. Swearing at the chain, Caleb considered what it would take to break it. He studied the way it was attached to the metal post and wondered if he could pull the metal post out quietly. Asshole and his crew weren't taking any chances in what they considered their property, and somehow that dog, as far as this asshole was concerned, was his.

Caleb looked around the area, still in hiding, figuring out the layout here, when a guard approached the dogs.

He threw in chunks of meat, and the four dogs ripped it to shreds. Caleb didn't know what kind of meat it was, but, in his heart, he was afraid it was a leg bone, as in, a human leg bone. He swore at that thought. Then the guard came over to look at the injured dog and laughed. He had a rifle over his shoulder. He sneered. "You'll be fed to the dogs next," he said. "Piece of shit, you are. And he had such high hopes for you."

The guard shook his head and went to pick up a stick to beat the dog with it. The dog snarled and tried to fight back, but he was badly enough injured that the guard landed the first blow on Beowulf, but, before the second blow made contact, Caleb ran an arm lock around the guard's neck, shutting off his voice, as he dragged him into the brush at the far corner of the dog pen out of sight. He knocked him out, at least he thought, but the guy jumped to his feet.

But when Caleb hit him the second time, he went down, hitting several small rocks. This time he stayed down. Caleb bent and placed a finger on his neck and realized that the guy's neck had snapped with the fall. Caleb tried to feel sympathy for him, but it was a struggle. Caleb took up the dead guy's rifle, put it over his shoulder, and grabbed the guy's shirt, putting it over his, disguising himself as the guard. Caleb grabbed the guy's hat too. Caleb checked the guard's pockets for keys and found some, hopefully for these pens. Luckily one of them opened Beowulf's pen where he'd been placed.

Caleb casually walked to the injured dog, whistling to him ever-so-softly, hopefully to stop him from panicking over the guard's outfit, and slowly bent and undid the collar around the dog's neck. The dog snarled and hissed at him, but Caleb kept talking to him in a long low calm voice. As soon as he had him free, Caleb called Beowulf to him.

The dog visibly hesitated, arguing with himself, but, considering this was his one chance at freedom, when Caleb walked out of the pen through the back gate, the dog came with him. After that, it was a matter of trying to get the dog to run. He watched Beowulf's progress, knowing he and the dog were in danger of being caught, and Caleb wouldn't likely be questioned but would take a bullet. Finally he reached down, not giving the dog any choice, picked him up in his arms, and raced toward the hillside.

But, as he bounced over the hilltop into the silence, behind him he heard a voice down below, yelling and raising the alarm. Now Caleb knew that the hunt would really be on. He stopped to catch his breath, and the dog looked up at him. Caleb put Beowulf down and asked, "Can you run?"

The dog whimpered, and Caleb nodded at him and said, "I know, but we got to do this, buddy. We got to do this." And together they headed cross-country on the far side and ran as far away from the men as he could and as far away from the tracks as he could. A creek was up ahead, and they needed that to help mess up their tracks—unless the bad guys had tracking dogs, and that would be bad news very quickly.

But now Caleb had some firepower, and that was a whole different ball game. With the dog at his side, they crossed the country as fast as their legs would carry them. Again he bent down, picked up the dog, and ran with him in his arms, but, this time, Caleb raced as fast as his legs would pelt out the miles underneath him—because he knew their time was up, and they would have men and dogs all over them in a heartbeat.

He crossed the creek, running downstream a good while—at least a mile, a mile and a half—and let the dog have a good drink. At that point in time, Caleb cooled down and had several drinks too. Then, on the other side, Beowulf seemed to pick up a little bit of energy. Both a little cooler now, they raced across the open field. Caleb had to get Beowulf to the trees on the other side, where they had cover. By the time they threw themselves into the copse on the other end, he heard voices.

He stopped to catch his breath and turned to look behind him. Men were in the bush on the far side, but nobody pointed in Caleb's direction. With the dog trembling at his side, Caleb had the two of them stay among the trees; he pulled out the rifle, using its site to figure out just how many were here. Three were on this side, and he couldn't see anybody else, except one had turned away and was walking back.

"Are they giving up?" he murmured. He hoped so, but he didn't expect it would be easy. If the bad guys gave up on this side, somebody would still come after Caleb and Beowulf on the other side of the border. This asshole's operation was that big to warrant this, in Caleb's mind, not even knowing for sure what the asshole did. Caleb didn't know how to get out of this permanently. But he had to get the dog out of here because it would be the next to die. No doubt that it already had been marked for the kill. And, even worse, Beowulf would be fed to his comrades out there.

Caleb waited and watched, but it looked like they were in the clear. He quickly sent a text to Laysha. **Out free and clear.** She immediately responded with a thumbs-up. He smiled at that. He texted back. **Give me 25.**

She gave him another happy emoji, and he turned to look at the dog and said, "Now we need to get the hell out of here for good." But the dog, at this point, no longer fought him and seemed to trust him, which was a good thing, because they had a long way to go, and Caleb needed that assist. With the dog in tow and him watching every step they made, the two of them headed toward the cantina. He was afraid to come in too close and wondered seriously about looking for another location. Just when he decided that was the answer, a truck drove past, close enough that he saw it was full of gunmen.

Instead of texting, he grabbed his phone, called her, and said, "Get out of there now."

"Where do you want to meet up now?" she said calmly.

He thought about it for a second and said, "Head to the

border."

"I'm not going home without you," she said.

"Head to the border, and I'll call you with a new location," he said. "We're surrounded by gunmen everywhere. I need you out of that cantina and fast."

"I already am. As soon as you told me to move, I moved."

He could feel some of his stress draining away. "Good, head back to the border. I'll circle around and see what other location we can arrange for a pickup."

"What shape is the dog in?" she murmured.

"Not good, his back end is injured," he said.

"Poor thing."

"Even worse, I think the man they shot and killed was fed to the other dogs."

"Oh, God," she breathed into the phone.

"I think Beowulf was marked for being food the next time too."

"But that's so wrong," she said.

"Maybe, but that's where we're at." He studied the country around him. "I'll go cross-country and head for the bush and see if I can come back around on the border."

"A lot of ranch territories around here."

"There is, and that's good because we need as much open space as we can get," he said.

"Okay, I'll drive toward home," she said. "I'll find a place to settle in off to the side. As soon as you have some idea where to pick you up, let me know."

"Will do," he said, and, at that, he hung up. He turned to look at the dog and asked, "You ready, Beowulf?" The dog looked up at him and gave a tiny sharp bark. "Good enough," he said. "Let's go."

And he picked up the pace and headed toward Texas. They had a lot of miles to go, and cross-country would be the easiest on both of them. He just wanted to make sure that Laysha got out of there safe and sound.

Otherwise he'd have another reason to come back and to really raise Cain. Caleb had hoped to get the dog away and to leave the asshole alone. Set the cops on him maybe, if that would do any good. But, if that asshole touched Laysha? Well, all bets were off. Caleb would go in and make sure every one of them paid.

CHAPTER 13

LAYSHA HAD MADE it sound like all was fine, but it certainly wasn't. She was being followed, and she didn't like it one bit. It didn't seem to matter what she did, she couldn't shake him. She didn't know who it was or why he was following her, but absolutely nothing good was about this scenario. As she headed toward the border and flew across it, the white truck came into Texas right behind her. She headed through some of the busiest areas of town, pulled in through parking lots and back out into main streets, doing anything she could to shake him. And just no luck. She swore, pulled into a busy restaurant, and sat in the parking lot.

The vehicle pulled in and parked near her. And it sat, just waiting. She didn't even know what to do. She wanted to ask for assistance, but she wouldn't leave the truck and her dogs. Yet sitting here made her an easy target too. She waited and watched to see what her stalker would do and then wondered if she could get close enough that she could get a picture of the driver. She pulled out her phone and set it to Camera. With the dogs lying confused beside her, she hit Reverse and backed up until she was parked crossways, right in front of his cab, and started taking photos.

At that, the vehicle drove forward, hitting her driver's side door.

She just smiled and took more photos as he yelled at her. She took as many as she wanted, knowing that the rental vehicle would take a beating. She hoped that Caleb had taken insurance out on it. But the noise he created had others coming out of the restaurant to see what was going on. And, with that, she pulled forward, toward several men. She stopped and pointed out the vehicle that had followed her, yelling, "That vehicle followed me all the way from Mexico, and I am terrified."

The men immediately headed for the truck, and, as if seeing that the tide had changed in her favor, the driver hit Reverse and took off. The men came racing back. One said, "I'm a cop. Did you get any photos of them?"

She nodded, immediately typing in his email address as he spouted it off for her. She quickly texted him several of the best of the photos. She looked at him with relief. "Oh, my God," she said, "I was so scared, I didn't know where to go."

"Well, that was pretty brave what you did," the cop said. "Some people would say it was also stupid as hell."

She winced. "I know. I just didn't know what else to do. I figured, if I went home, he'd follow me there, and that was the last thing I wanted."

"Well, we've got photos, and we certainly have witnesses now. Plus, his front end is damaged, from hitting your rental," he said. "I'm putting out a BOLO to see if we can get the guy picked up. You'll need to come to the station so we can file a report."

"Then you want to watch the border," she said. "I wondered if it had something to do with that murder in that empty house."

He looked at her in surprise. "What do you know about

it?"

"I was one of the pair who found the body," she said, shaking. "And, ever since then, I've had several strangers come to my house in the middle of the night, and one shot at us." She mentioned the detective's name handling the case.

"He's a friend of mine. I'll contact him."

"Could you do that?" she asked. "I'm starting to go into shock, I think." She held up her hand, shivering badly.

"Go home," he said. "We'll contact you there. You'll be fine."

"Maybe," she said, but she knew she couldn't go home until she picked up Caleb. "Maybe I'll drive somewhere and get a coffee. I'm scared to go home now."

He nodded. "Hopefully we'll find this guy right away. I'll contact Ansel, and we'll get back to you about it."

"Good," she said. "I hadn't realized, but a friend of mine said that the rental house backed up to the house owned by that nasty drug-running, dog-killing, women-selling asshole on the Mexican border."

"Huevo?"

"Yeah, apparently. I looked it up on the map, and the properties back up to each other."

He stared at her in surprise, his look calculating. A thought then came into his head. "You know, that almost makes sense."

"Well, I'm not sure," she said. "I wasn't thinking anything about it. I drove past the place because I felt so bad for the dead guy," she said. "Then I remembered what my friend said."

"I'll have to look into that," he said. "We've been after that Huevo asshole for a long time."

"When I was just there at the nearby property, I heard gunfire," she said. "I don't know how long it takes to hear gunfire, but I was just walking around the back of the rental property, and I heard something in the distance."

"Huevo's wanted for at least a half-dozen murders. We've just never found any proof of any bodies."

"Well, if he keeps a pack of dogs, I wouldn't be at all surprised if he feeds the dead people to the dogs," she snapped. "He's just an asshole to do that."

"That would be wrong," he said, "but it's not a bad idea."

"It's a terrible idea," she said. "Those poor dogs."

"Maybe," he murmured. "But it's smart on the criminal's part."

"Maybe, but just to think of him doing that? I mean, the animals wouldn't know the difference between what they're eating, and they would be quite happy to chow down on some guy just because this asshole doesn't like them."

"Very true," he said. "Go home. We'll handle it."

"Okay," she said with relief, and she pulled away and slowly drove forward. She'd given him as much information as she dared, without getting Caleb into trouble. And, even so, it wasn't that easy. She wanted to call Caleb and to see how he was doing but didn't want to get him into more trouble by calling him at the wrong time. But no way in hell was she going home. Not now. Not with this going on.

Not without Caleb.

CALEB KNEW HE'D put at least ten miles on his body because he could feel it. His joints screamed, and his injuries ached, but, as he looked down at Beowulf beside him, the dog was in worse shape, and he was still going strong. Caleb loved that grit, and this animal was game for whatever, as long as it got him out of that hellhole. As they traveled, Caleb talked to Beowulf, asking him how the hell he got into that mess.

The dog barked every once in a while, making Caleb laugh. He could feel something going on in the background of the world around him, as if his instincts were saying that trouble was up ahead.

He pulled out his phone and, without breaking stride, texted Laysha, asking if she was okay. She sent back a quick message.

Yes.

But it came back short and fast and made him nervous. He called her, trying hard to keep his breathing even. "Are you sure you're okay?" he asked.

"I am now," she said with relief. "Am I glad to hear you."

"What happened?" he asked.

"I was followed," she said and quickly explained what had happened.

He could feel his insides congeal. "Now that's not good news," he snapped.

"I don't want anyone following us home," she said, "but I did end up getting some help from people standing nearby, and I was lucky enough that a cop was one of them."

"Good," he said. "I'll send a message to Ansel and ask him to look into it," he said.

"I also told the cop about the shot that I heard. He said they'd been after the asshole for several murders but hadn't found any bodies."

"That'll be an interesting thing to consider," he said quietly.

"Well, I hope so. I didn't want to let on what we were doing, and I didn't want the dog to be brought up, in case you wanted to keep that out of the news. But I did want the cops aware that the property with the dead guy was really close to this asshole Huevo's compound."

"Right, and that's a good point," he murmured.

"Are you running?"

"Yes, the two of us are."

"Oh, good," she said. "I thought the dog was too badly hurt."

"Yes, and no," he said. "His back end is hurt, but we're moving because we have to. We both know that, so no discussion is required."

"I love that," she said, "how that's not an option in your world."

"It isn't," he said, "but it is a little harder to talk at the same time.'"

"I'll hang up."

"No," he said, "it's good to hear from you."

"Well, it's good to hear from you too because I'm worried about you," she said. "At the same time, I don't know where to go and meet you."

"And I don't want you going home if I'm not there," he said. "Depends if they know who you are."

"No reason for them to," she said.

"Maybe, but you know they're smarter than we like to give them credit for."

"They're also assholes," she said, "and believe me. As soon as I get home, I'll be grabbing that rifle of mine."

"And keep it close," he murmured. "Make sure you keep it close."

Putting his phone away, Caleb kept moving, feeling the miles eat away at his endurance. When he finally came to another creek, he immediately soaked his face deep in the water. The back of his head was in the water, as Beowulf moved into the creek beside him, lapping up and drinking to his heart content. "Not too much, boy. When we get moving again, it'll be hard to run with full bellies."

The dog looked at him but continued to drink.

Caleb knew how Beowulf felt. As Caleb oriented himself in his new location, he realized there was a good chance he'd already crossed the border. Moving out at a slower pace, he headed toward the closest highway.

He used the GPS on his phone and sent several messages to Badger, looking for directions, depending on where he was going. When he heard a vehicle, he stopped, hiding himself and Beowulf for a moment, and headed in the direction of the vehicle. What he needed to do was find out where he was and ensure it was safe for her to come get him here.

As they came upon one of the main highways, a gas station and a big pullout was up ahead. He moved cautiously forward, even as he dialed her. When there was no answer, he frowned, hung up, and then tried again.

Almost immediately she answered this time.

"There you are," he said. "When you didn't answer, I got worried."

"I'm here," she said. "Where are you?"

"There's a gas station, but I'm not exactly sure what road I'm on," he said. "I'll talk to somebody to see where I am, but I have a general idea. I think I'm heading into town but about ten miles out."

"Could you have traveled that far?"

"Oh, yeah," he said. "I've done at least twelve miles, if not fifteen. I don't want to push the dog too much more."

"How is Beowulf?"

"Hurt but game," he said. "That's all that I care about right now."

"Right," she said. "Well, I can head in your direction, so at least I'll be close enough whenever you can figure it out."

"I'll see if Badger can track my phone," he said. "Then I'll give you better directions."

"No problem," she said.

When they hung up, he moved cautiously toward the gas station up ahead. It was a big one, and he looked down at the dog, already hesitant about going forward. He reached out and gently stroked the dog on the head. "It'll be fine. Honest. We'll make sure that you're not in any trouble this time."

And it wasn't the dog's fault last time; Caleb still didn't know what had happened. When he got to the side of the gas station, he picked a shady spot off one corner and sat down, his hands gently smoothing the dog's head, trying to calm him down. He had his hackles up, as he stared at the people moving around him.

"Not everybody is like that," he murmured to the dog. The dog leaned against his hand, pushing his body weight against him. Emboldened by that, Caleb gently ran his hands over the dog, giving him orders to lift his paws, so that he could check them. Some of the pads were bleeding from the rough run. "You've been out of training, haven't you?"

The dog looked at him, then rubbed his head against Caleb's chin. Taking just a few minutes to relax and to bond, he ran his hands over the dog, until he got to the dog's back end, where the dog immediately growled.

"I hear you," he said, "but we'll have to get that checked out." He then ordered the dog to stand still, and the dog immediately complied, and he ran his hands gently over him to see what was going on. The leg wasn't broken, but, if he wasn't mistaken, it looked like a huge bullet burn ran along the dog's back. It was deep and angry looking, if not infected. He sighed. "Did he already try to shoot you, buddy? That's one asshole who needs some of his own medicine, if that's how he thinks to treat a dog."

After checking all four feet, making sure there were no other injuries, Caleb came back to give that wound a closer look. It needed stitching, if it were even possible to stitch at this point. It looked like the bullet had torn some muscle and done a fair bit of damage. Caleb came back around, gently stroking the dog on the head and the nose. "It's okay," he said. "You will heal. You might not be as pretty as you were before, but it's okay because you'll make it now."

Beowulf leaned into him. There was no sign of a big aggressive dog at this point. But there shouldn't be at any time with a military dog, unless he was on command for attack. In this case, the dog was just looking for a chance to get back to a normal life. To some human interaction. Whatever that would mean for him. He had to be shocked and scared by all that had changed.

Now rested, Caleb assessed several other people coming in and out of the gas station. An older man walked a small dachshund over to the trees. Stashing the weapon in the bushes and keeping Beowulf close to his side, knowing he didn't have a leash but holding him on orders to stay, Caleb approached the older man.

The man looked at him in surprise and looked at the dog. "Wow, that's a good-size animal," he said. "Old pudgy here, he would not be anything but a tiny morsel for him."

"Well, the good news is," Caleb said, "Beowulf doesn't eat morsels like that."

The old man nodded, and a little bit of relief passed over his face. "I'm sure he needs to lift the leg just as much as mine does."

"That he does," he said. "We're a little bit lost too."

"Oh, well, you're only about ten miles out of El Paso," he said. "The city limits are probably only about eight miles from here." He pointed at the highway. "Just drive on down there, and you can't miss it, biggest damn city around," he muttered. "My wife, she insisted on coming here and living close to her relatives, whereas I'd rather be a long way off," he said, shaking his head.

From the far corner, somebody, a woman, yelled, "Henry!"

He rolled his eyes and said, "Sometimes I wonder if I shouldn't be a long way away from her too." But tugging his little dog, he moved in the direction of his wife.

With that information, Caleb quickly sent a message to Laysha, telling her where he was. He barely sent off those text messages when Badger called him. "Are you at the gas station just outside El Paso?" he asked. "We've got your phone at that location."

"Yes, I'm sitting in the parking lot now," he said. "I just sent Laysha a message to come my way."

"How's the dog?"

"He's holding. Needs to see a vet. It looks like he's been shot along the back, starting at his haunch. It's a deep gouge, and it's ugly. I don't know if it's too late for stitches or not," he said, "but I'll get him to a vet here pretty quick. Under the circumstances …" Caleb filled in Badger with the ugly details. "I'm pretty damn sure they murdered the guy and then fed him to the dogs."

"Oh, God," Badger said. "I wonder how often that happens on that property."

"Probably often. The dogs are all so badly treated," he said, "but not as bad as anybody who works for this asshole."

"So we'll have to take a look at that too," he said. "We can't just rescue the one dog and leave the rest."

"I'm not sure if they'll be salvageable or not," he warned.

"No, I hear you," he said. "It's one of the things that we'll have to figure out. But I've got calls into the cops now," he said. "I'll follow-up right now with that information."

"Good enough." As he hung up, Caleb heard a honk, and he looked over to see Laysha driving toward him in the rental. He lifted a hand, realizing he'd never seen anything quite so nice as the smile on her face when she caught sight of him.

Life was damn good. He could only hope now that maybe there was some hope of a future for them both. Because he didn't want to lose any of what he just now had finally gained. His brother be damned. Jackson could have Caleb's ex-wife. Laysha was on Caleb's horizon. And she was worth waiting for.

CHAPTER 14

LAYSHA DROVE STRAIGHT toward him, overwhelmed to see him safe and sound. She studied the dog as she drove into the parking lot. He looked like he'd been through a rough couple months. But she also saw something so majestic within him that her heart broke when she thought about what he must have gone through at the hands of that asshole.

She pulled in to the side and parked. She let the dogs out, hoping that was okay, managing to clip the leash on her three rather excited ones, whereas Graynor was always well behaved. Graynor walked up wearily to the side of Caleb, studying the other dog lying at Caleb's side.

Beowulf's ears were up, and he studied Graynor with interest. Obviously recognizing a kindred soul of some kind. When Graynor arrived with the three yappy things, Beowulf seemed to accept that they were part of the pack. Graynor walked over, and the two big dogs sniffed. No animosity, no anger. As if one old soldier recognized a wounded one. Laysha walked over, and Caleb stood and opened his arms. She raced into them, and, when they closed around her, she whispered, "I was so scared for you."

"For me?" he said. "How do you think I felt, knowing some asshole followed you?"

She smiled. "I got rid of him though," she said, "but it

took the cops and the other guys to do it."

"I'm just sorry it had to happen that way at all," he said gruffly. "Not very good on my part."

"Why do you figure?" She looked up at him carefully. "You can't protect everyone all the time."

He squeezed her and tugged her back into his arms. "Maybe not," he said, "but I sure as hell don't want to see you going through that again."

"Hey, I'm right with you there on that one," she said. She stopped, crouched in front of the War Dog, and gently offered the back of her hand for the dog to staff. He sniffed, and his tail wagged ever-so-slightly. "How's he been?"

"Well, he's sore. He's tired. He needs a vet to make sure that that hindquarter will be okay. I think it's infected. Maybe a bullet burned through the muscle," he said. "I've checked it out as much as I can, but it needs a good wash. We might have to sedate him for that."

"Poor thing," she murmured. "You sure it's him?"

"Yes, while I was sitting here, I sent images of the tattoos to Badger, and it's Beowulf. The vet should check the microchip on him, but, as far as I'm concerned, this is Beowulf."

The dog lifted his head in their direction at his name.

"Even his markings are fairly identifiable," she said, studying the irregular brown-black pattern on his ears. "I feel so bad for him," she murmured. "And for the other dogs."

"I know," he said. He stared at Beowulf. "Do you have a vet?"

She nodded. "And he does house calls."

Caleb frowned at that and said, "I don't know if we can knock him out and do whatever is needed on a house call, can we?"

"Let's phone and ask," she said. She pulled out her phone and phoned her favorite vet. When Sandy the receptionist answered, Laysha explained what the problem was.

"As long as it's not major surgery, then the vet can come fully equipped, yes," she said, "but, if we've got to give him general anesthesia and knock him out, then we need to keep him here."

"Maybe it'd be better to run him down there right now," she said, "if you guys have time to take a look at him."

"That would probably be best. Let me check the schedule." She came back and said, "We can squeeze you in at the end of the day."

"Which is only what? Half an hour?" she said in a note of humor.

"Make it an hour," Sandy said.

"Good enough," she said, putting away her phone, as she relayed the message to Caleb.

He nodded and said, "That's not bad. We're maybe twenty minutes from there anyway?"

"Given the rush-hour traffic now, if we went straight there, we'd be lucky to make it," she said with a wry twist. "El Paso is not exactly a small town anymore."

"Not sure it ever was," he said. "Let's head over and see if we can get all the dogs into the truck as it is."

She nodded. "You drive. I'll take the three little ones upfront. Do you think Graynor and Beowulf would be all right to take over the back seat?"

"I think so," he said. "You put Graynor in first."

She walked around to the side and opened up the far passenger door, ordering Graynor up. The huge German wirehaired pointer hopped up lightly and settled on the cushion. She closed the door, loaded the three little ones into her front passenger area, two on their feet with Fancy in her arms, while Caleb slowly ordered Beowulf into the back. The dog had no trouble getting to the bottom footwell but struggled to get up on the seat. Gently giving him a hand, Caleb raised him onto the seat, lay the rifle on the floor and closed the door. He came around to the driver's side, hopped in, and said, "Well, we got a houseful."

"A ready-made family," she said lightly.

"This kind I can handle," he said with a grin.

She smiled at that and settled in for the drive.

She was right. The traffic was pretty rough. There was not only construction but also an accident. She wondered if she should phone and say they were coming, but she had been held up tending to the dogs, and then they pulled in just a minute late. As they slowly unpacked all the dogs, Laysha walked up to the front door, and Sandy saw her, now unlocking the door to bring her in.

"I was afraid you wouldn't make it," she said.

"So were we. The construction, the traffic, and then an accident caused quite a snarl," she said.

The receptionist nodded. "It seems like there's always something on the road these days."

"I know. I'm just grateful I wasn't part of the accident," she said.

"It's always that way, isn't it? You get angry and frustrated at the beginning, and then immediately common sense kicks in and says, *Hey, at least it wasn't you out there.*"

"And then you wonder if one day it'll be you," she said. She held open the door as Beowulf walked in slowly, dragging that back leg a bit.

Sandy looked at him and said, "Wow, he looks exhausted."

"He's run over twelve miles with me today," Caleb said.

She looked at him sharply. "Why would you do that to an injured dog?"

"To save the dog's life," he said briefly.

Once again Laysha realized how little he expected or intended to explain himself. He did when he felt it was necessary, and, if she—or others—didn't like it, that was just too bad. Laysha looked at Sandy, seeing the doubt on her face, and Laysha nodded. "Trust me. The dog was in a really ugly position. We were trying to save him before he was shot and fed to other dogs."

The shock on the woman's face helped to diffuse her initial anger a little bit. She immediately headed to the back room to let the vet know. Charlie came out on her heels, smiling that big affable smile that Laysha had become so accustomed to. He looked at her and grinned. "Brought me another one, did you? Keeping this one too?"

She chuckled. "Not sure I'm allowed to." She stepped back, after introducing Charlie to Caleb.

Caleb quickly explained about the War Dog.

At that, the vet crouched in front of the dog with interest. "Haven't seen one of these guys before," he said. "I heard a couple of my cohorts have. How I always wanted to meet one too, though he looks like he's been run through the mill and back."

"Exactly," Caleb said, "we also had to do a twelve-mile run cross-country to get away from bullets."

"It's never easy, is it?" he said. "Come on. Let's get him into the back."

And, with that, Caleb and Beowulf disappeared with Charlie. Sandy looked over at Laysha. "Seriously that dog ran twelve miles?"

"They're both veterans," she said with a sideways look at her. "Caleb has been medically discharged from the military. I believe that the twelve-mile run would have hit both of them pretty hard."

"Jeez," she said. She walked around to the front desk. "I have no idea what something like this will cost," she said apologetically, "and I've pretty well shut down the system for the day."

"Not a problem." Then she added, "You know I'm good for it."

"You do take good care of all those other dogs," she said, "and I can't believe Graynor is still doing as well as he is."

"I hope I never lose him," she said. "He's very special to me."

"I hear you, but at that one point in time …"

"I know. Everybody keeps saying that, but he keeps surprising me."

"He could go another couple years," she said.

"I hope so. He's been a huge part of my life."

"I hear that," she said. "We have so many dogs through here, and we're having to put down so many lately. It's very distressing."

"Do you give them to rescues?"

"We try to find a rescue that can take them. Believe me. Nothing breaks my heart more than to put down a healthy dog. So we work hard to place them," she said. "But sometimes there's just nothing we can do."

"I've often wondered if I should open up a rescue myself," she said, "but I'm afraid I'll be inundated with dogs that I won't want to give up."

"Anytime you want to open your heart and your door,"

Sandy said, "let me know. Because sometimes the stories are just enough to break all our hearts."

"I have a home myself now," she said, "and five acres."

"That's enough room to take in some strays," she said, "but, when you think about it, we all need space and food to feed them too."

"Exactly." Laysha sat down in the waiting room with her four. They hated the vet's office, like most animals. Graynor sat very close to her, but she kept a hand on his head and neck, gently stroking him. "It's okay, buddy. We're not here for you. It's Beowulf that's struggling."

By the time Caleb came out, a serious look was on his face.

"I don't like that look," she said, hopping to her feet. "How is he?"

"Well, the bullet did a little more damage than I suspected," he said. "They'll keep him here overnight, and we'll see what he's like in the morning."

"Stitches, surgery?"

"Both. We just got the bullet out, but we had to knock him out." He showed her a small pill bottle with the bullet in it. "For the cops."

"So that makes sense to keep him overnight then," she said, frowning. "I wish Beowulf didn't have to though. I wanted him to come home."

"You and me both," he said.

"But they don't generally keep him if nobody's here."

Caleb nodded. "The vet said he had another overnight patient, so he was staying here anyway. So it just made sense to keep Beowulf too."

"Fine," she said, not liking the decision.

He smiled at her and said, "Any reason not to keep him

here?"

"Only that I'm a mother hen," she said, "and I don't want to see him left alone."

"Oh, don't even bring up the tear-jerker stuff. I'm leaving the dog here," he said, "and you know that I'm really not good with that."

"I know," she said, giving him a cheeky grin. "You'd put a cot in the same room and stay here too, if the vet would let you."

He looked at her, his lips quirking. "The trouble is, I know you would too."

"Yep," she said, "furry family *is* family."

"Yeah, but you keep making me expand mine to include humankind."

She laughed out loud at that. "I do, indeed, but you will survive."

"How about these guys? Do they need anything while we're here?"

"To leave," she said bluntly. "This is not their favorite location."

"Well, just like doctors and hospitals aren't any place that most of us like," he said, "Beowulf has taken it fairly well. But he's sleeping solidly now."

"And he needs that as much as anything," she said. "It was a pretty rough ride home."

"I know, and I need to go home and rest myself," he admitted.

"Good enough," she said.

They say goodbye to the receptionist, who was even now locking up the office. Laysha reloaded her dogs and they headed home again.

"I sure hope we have food at home for dinner," she said,

yawning. "We missed lunch."

"Well, we had lunch or brunch or whatever," he said, "but it's well past dinnertime, and we need to get home and get another coat on that floor."

She groaned. "God," she said, "not sure I have the energy for that."

"We'll check it out when we get home," he said, "but I suspect that it'll be more than ready for the next coat."

"Wouldn't be so bad just putting down another coat," she said, "but we got to sand it first."

"And the sanding, as you well know, gives it such a perfect finish."

"It doesn't matter how much you're trying to make me feel better about doing this," she said, "it's still a lot of work."

He chuckled. "It is, indeed, and you love every minute of it."

"Except when I'm exhausted," she admitted.

He looked at her and asked, "Over the shock of being followed and alone?"

"I will be fine," she said with a shrug. "It is what it is."

"Maybe, but that isn't necessarily an easy thing to go through."

"No, it sure wasn't." Changing subjects, she said, "I'm sure we can find something to eat. If we find some energy, we will do the floor. If not," she murmured, "I'm heading straight to bed." And to emphasize her words, she yawned a huge noisy yawn. She collapsed against the seat.

"I think it's more the stress than anything. That's usually the killer," he said in agreement.

As he drove back home carefully, she looked around. "Do you always now look behind you to see if we're being followed?"

"Unfortunately, yes," he said with a nod. "Not the way you want to live, but, after you've been followed once and gotten through a scary scenario, you always wonder, worry, if it's happening."

As he drove up to the house, she looked and said, "And you set it up so that we'd know if somebody was here while we were gone, right?"

He nodded. He helped her out of the vehicle and waited while she got all the animals and walked up to the front. He checked the front door and then held up a hand to stop.

She looked at him and whispered, "What's the matter?"

"You've had an uninvited visitor."

SHE STARED AT him, while he checked. Then he turned and looked at her and said, "I'll take Graynor with me, but I want you and the other dogs to stay here, while I do a check of the house and bring my rifle inside."

She nodded slowly. "You want to bring my shotgun back down when you come?" she murmured.

"Will do," he said. And, with that, he disappeared inside. He checked the living room and made a quick pass through the entire downstairs, thinking he heard something upstairs. He looked down at Graynor. "What do you think, bud?" Graynor sat at the base of the stairs, staring upward. Caleb nodded. "Yeah, that's my take too."

He studied the stairs, the old handrails and banisters might squeak, but the base that they were on should be solid. He moved slowly toward the stairs and then climbed them. He motioned for Graynor to stay, but the dog wasn't having anything to do with it, which meant there really was a threat upstairs.

Worried that Laysha would come in after him, he quickly sent her a text to stay outside and to stay hidden from sight. He moved slowly and steadily up the stairs. As soon as he could peek around the landing, he shuffled onto the railing, grabbed a hold of the upper railing on the second floor, and pulled himself up and over at the same time.

Graynor burst up onto the second floor. He stood and waited, his back against the wall between two doors. But nothing opened; all the doors upstairs were closed. Good move because it'd be easier to check exactly where somebody was as they moved through the house. He watched as Graynor sniffed from one door to the next, and, at the master, he stopped and growled.

Caleb tapped his nose to stop.

That was good enough for Caleb. He immediately opened the door silently on the left, checked it out, and then on the right. He knew Graynor was correct, but Caleb wanted to make sure he didn't miss anything. He didn't want to get a surprise attack from behind. A further check of the bathroom showed that it was equally empty. That meant everybody was waiting in the master. He thought about that for a long moment.

He had a good idea of the layout of the master. There was no way for her to get in or out, which is what had been the problem when redoing the floors. Casually he noted that the floors were ready for the next coat.

But now they had somebody hiding in her master. And that just pissed him right off. The fact that somebody had entered her house was one thing; the fact that somebody waited in her bedroom was an entirely different thing. Both were inexcusable, but this one just added to the injury.

Caleb thought about the windows outside, wondering if he could sneak in somewhere along the line. He remembered her comment about wanting to get one of those drop-down ladders, something he should have looked at a little earlier. But they were trying to get the floors finished first.

He studied the attic access above and realized that he could probably jump up and pull himself into the attic cutout. However, if he couldn't get through to her bedroom from the attic, what good would it do? He frowned as he thought about it, and then Graynor growled again, his voice rising.

On instinct, Caleb dove for the big dog and pulled him away from the door to the master. At the same instant bullets fired through the door and would have hit the dog right where he was. The dog froze in his arms, the two of them waiting for the bullet shower to stop, hoping Laysha stayed outside. She would have heard the whole mess, and the last thing he wanted was for her to barge in. He quickly sent her a text, saying the shooter was in her room, and they were both unharmed. She sent back a thumbs-up and a note saying she was calling 9-1-1. He pulled up Ansel's number and sent him a text.

Caleb didn't want the intruder inside to know they were here. Caleb wanted the shooter to open the damn door to see if he got everybody or anybody for that matter. Particularly the dog. Everybody around here seemed to be dog haters, and that made Caleb angry too. At that thought, he heard a footstep inside; he reached down and pinched Graynor's jaws together, warning him not to bark or growl. They had to be silent. The last thing Caleb wanted was for this guy to realize his enemy still waited.

Right now Caleb was in a tough spot because he didn't know who was on the other side, and he wouldn't know until the shooter actually opened the door. As the footsteps cautiously came forward, Graynor stiffened. Caleb gently stroked him and pet him, trying to ease his fear, with his own gun out and ready. The two waited in silence. Caleb patted him gently, hoping the gunman didn't have Laysha's shotgun or .22 rifle. He didn't want that much firepower against him.

As the footsteps reached the door, he could almost hear the gunman bending down, trying to see through the bullet holes. But it was pretty hard to see; there was enough shattered wood to make that an impossibility. And finally Caleb stood up slowly, not daring to breathe, waiting, because he knew the guy inside just couldn't wait to figure out where the dog was at. And suddenly the door burst open and out came the handgun first.

Caleb jumped, his right leg kicking the handgun away, while grabbing the man in a chokehold, and dumped him on the floor. Then he called out, "Graynor, guard."

Immediately Graynor came forward, sat beside the guy, leaning into the shooter's face and growling deeply.

The guy started screaming. "Get him off me. Get him off me."

"Hell no," Caleb said, "you just tried to shoot him."

"I didn't. I didn't," he said. "It was an accident."

"You're a fucking asshole. Of course you shot at my dog," he sneered. "We don't really like animal abusers around this place. Besides, what are you doing in this house in the first place?"

"I got lost," he said. "I didn't know anybody lived here. I came in to check it out, but there was nobody to ask."

"Right," Caleb said, "try another excuse. You're trespassing, and you know what we do to trespassers in this state?"

"Don't shoot," he roared.

"No, hell no, I don't need to shoot," he said, "but you can bet that the cops won't give a shit."

"No, no, no, no," he said. "I'll pay you to let me go."

"You can't pay me enough to let you go," he said, "but I'd be happy to let you run because I'm more than happy to shoot you on your way out my door. You entered these premises illegally. You fired upon us illegally, and you tried to kill my dog in his own home," he said. "As far I'm concerned, you're done for."

"No," the guy cried out.

At that, Caleb eased back ever-so-slightly and turned him over onto his back, so he saw his face. Immediately he took photos and sent them to Badger and to Ansel. And then he sent it to Laysha.

She opened the front door and called out, "Can I come up?"

"Yes, carefully," he said. "I've got your intruder here."

She came racing up with the other dogs. She stopped with a gasp. "Oh my," she said, "that's the guy who followed me in the white pickup."

Caleb looked down at the shooter in shock. "This asshole?"

"Yes, he's the one who followed me from the cantina."

"I don't know you," the stranger snapped. "I don't know anything about you."

Laysha pulled out her phone and showed Caleb the photos she'd taken. "Ansel was looking for him already."

"Well, that's good. Then we can tell him that we've got him. So now we have a stalker charge, and the B&E, and the shooting charge too."

"Well, I doubt he has a license for that weapon," she said. "Guys like him never do."

The intruder dropped his act and sneered at her. "What do you mean, *guys like me?*" he asked. "You'll never fucking hold me. I'll be out in no time."

"Well, thanks for the warning," she murmured. Sirens were in the distance as she looked over at Caleb. "You okay if I go down and let them in?"

"Yeah, absolutely," he said. "I'm just waiting for this guy to run."

"I'm not running anywhere," he said. "You're not shooting me in the back. That's not any way for any man to die."

"And yet, that's how you killed the man in the rental house," she shot back as she turned and left.

The look of stark fear on the guy's face made Caleb sit back. He murmured, "So she was right? Interesting that. We'll have to make sure forensics has a really good chance to match you up. Now you look incredibly nervous."

"I didn't do anything," he said.

"Well, the cops will let us know that pretty damn fast," he said. "Pretty stupid location though for a body drop. Why the hell would you leave a dead body at the other guy's house?"

He didn't say anything.

"Don't talk. I don't care," he said. "That's the detective's issue."

"No detectives," he said.

"Too damn late," Ansel said as he climbed the stairs. "We really don't like stalkers and people who attack women in this town."

"I didn't attack anybody," he said.

Ansel rose to the top of the stairs and looked down at the scene in front of him. "Wow," he said. "I half expected to see the War Dog with you."

"Yeah, well, that War Dog's at the vet's," Caleb said, "partly because of this asshole." He handed over the bullet the vet had given him, then the casings he'd found in the back of Laysha's property. He'd email the pictures later. "I'm sure you can match that to the bullet your team collected from the wall here."

"We will, but it doesn't happen overnight." He pocketed the evidence. "So this is the guy, huh?"

The guy immediately shook his head. "I don't know anything about what you're talking about," he said, "and I certainly don't know what a War Dog is."

"It's the dog you had tied up at your boss's place. You know? The dog you shot."

"I didn't shoot a dog," he said. "That was the boss."

"Well, was it the boss who just shot the man at his place? Because I saw him do it. Then chopped him up and fed him to the damn dogs."

"That's his method," he said, his voice very, very quiet. "You don't want to mess with him. You end up as dog food."

"Oh, I got that message," Caleb said quietly. "Do you realize you've already messed up? So you're next."

"No, no, I've worked with him for years," he said.

"You only get so many free passes," Caleb said. "You've had all of yours."

The guy looked at him in terror. "You don't understand. I mean, sometimes he doesn't fully kill the men before he gives them to the dogs. That's not humane. The boss is a psycho. I've seen him do it."

"Nobody wants that," he said. "You didn't do anything about it either, did you?"

"What do you want me to do?" he cried out. "Anybody who bucks him dies."

"Well, an awful lot of deaths are to be accounted for that happened in that house, not to mention the previous owners of the dog. Do you know anything about them? They appear to have disappeared," he said. When the man just stared at him in terror, he added, "And if you think you won't get caught along with Huevo, you're wrong."

"I haven't done anything," he said, his voice very, very low and ugly. "You can't make it look like I did."

"We already have you on three counts. Besides you screwed up because nobody was supposed to find that body for a long time."

"Nobody was supposed to find it," he said, "and that's the way it was supposed to be. Make sure all the evidence was gone. I wanted the body to be found sometime. Give the family closure."

"And why is that?"

"It's my cousin," he said resentfully. "I didn't want him eaten by the dogs. I figured at least he'd get buried this way eventually."

"And so you starved the dogs, huh?"

"No, they ate very well that day," he said bitterly. "Two men died, and my cousin was one of them. One man was the War Dog's previous owner. The woman was fed to them for dessert."

Caleb's stomach revolted. No wonder no one wanted to buck this guy. Fear was a hell of a motivator.

"What the hell makes you think that you're safe now?" Ansel asked, looking at him in surprise. "You've already been marked. We have you in custody. Huevo already knows that you've talked."

"No, no, no, no," he said. "He knows me."

"Yeah, that means he also knows how you felt about your cousin and that you screwed up on that because it's already all over the news that we found the body."

"If that's true, I'm dead."

"Well then, you better help us out so that we can pin him into a jail cell before he comes after you."

"There isn't a jail cell that'll hold him," he said wearily. "He's damn scary. He doesn't give a shit about anyone or anything. He kills the women if they don't make him happy."

"Can the dogs eat it all?" Ansel asked the intruder, but he was staring at Caleb.

That was something that bothered Caleb. Of course, anybody who knew that was their future wouldn't perform in any way that would make anybody happy. This Huevo guy was somebody who just wanted a reign of terror.

"Not always," he said. "Then the body parts go into the freezer. Over the next couple days they'll get another piece."

"Has he ever killed anybody because he ran out of dog food?" Caleb asked.

At that, Ansel looked over at him in surprise, and then his face twisted in horror.

"Yes," the intruder whispered. "One of the young women. She had a scar on her face, and he figured that she would be no good on the market."

"Great, and I wonder if it wasn't an asshole, like you, who put that scar on her face."

"It was him. He hit her too hard," he said, "and then he shot her. He didn't kill her though and fed her to the dogs anyway."

"Nice guy," Ansel said.

The intruder looked up at him, his eyes dark. "I've seen things," he said, shaking his head. "I still can't sleep at night."

"And that's how he functions, on complete terror."

"It's not fair," he said. "Some of those women, they didn't deserve it."

"And the men did?"

At that, he winced. "No," he said, "but they knew the game."

"And that makes a difference," Caleb said in acknowledgment.

"But not enough. You don't know him. He's got spies everywhere."

"Of course he does, that's how he keeps everyone obedient. So he already knows that you've been picked up."

"Not yet," he said, his voice exhausted, "but you're right. He will soon."

"So what can you do to help your case?"

"Nothing. If I go back now, he won't believe me, and, even if somebody tries to convince him otherwise, he won't believe them, and they'll get shot, so nobody'll even bother."

"Nice boss," he said.

"No, you have no idea," he whispered. He shook his head, laid back down, and stared up at the cops. "Just shoot me, please."

"No, I can't do that," Ansel said mildly. "But you can bet we'll take you to prison and will let everybody know where you are."

"I won't last a night," he said. "And that's a fact."

Ansel looked at the intruder intently.

"Of course, he already has several of the guards in his palm," Caleb said.

"Interesting," Ansel murmured.

"You guys have no idea how much corruption there is," the intruder said.

"Well, we have a good idea. We're getting a handle on it," he said.

"He grabs brothers, daughters, sisters, friends," he said. "He takes whoever you care about and holds them until he's got you where he wants you. Then and only then he releases them, if you're lucky. And, if you're lucky, he releases them alive. Otherwise, he just keeps them as a threat over your head."

"Is that what happened to you?"

"Yeah, my kid brother a long time ago," he said. "He was really sick and couldn't pay for the treatments he needed as he didn't have no insurance. So my agreement was, I work for Huevo and do his dirty jobs to keep my brother alive."

"And how long did that last?"

"My brother died about a year and a half later," he said, "but, by then, I was already in so deep."

"Did you ever wonder if he didn't kill your brother anyway?"

"I did wonder, and I have no proof," he said, "but it's something that eats away at me."

"How did your brother die?"

He looked at him. "A drive-by bullet."

"Well, that's pretty obvious."

"And still I can do nothing about it. He doesn't accept anything but blind loyalty. And no screw-ups."

"Can you identify the guys he's killed?" Ansel asked him.

"Some of them," he said. "Well, most of them probably."

"We'll need a list of those names," he said, "because, if nothing else, families are out there, looking for their loved ones."

"Won't even be anything left," he said. "Those dogs are so damn vicious."

"And, of course, they are more vicious because he keeps them half-starved."

"That's the only saving grace," the gunman said quietly. "At least for the people still alive when they go in. They die quickly."

"Well, the dogs will have to be put down. You know that."

"I do," he said, "and I, for one, would like to see it. I know that they didn't deserve it and all that jazz," he said, "but they're too far gone now."

"Good to know," Ansel said, as he looked at Caleb.

"There still could be a chance to save the dogs," Caleb said.

"You know what happens when you are after killer dogs."

He nodded. "I know. It just breaks my heart because it wasn't their fault."

"It isn't, but it is," the gunman said. "God, I'm so tired of this life. Good to know it will be over soon."

"Well, you could also do something right for a change, before it's over," the detective said.

He looked at him, smiled, and said, "If it takes down that asshole, fine, but I'm telling you that I won't live until tomorrow. So anything you want to know, you need to know tonight."

CHAPTER 15

LAYSHA WATCHED AS the detective marched the intruder outside onto the porch, where she stood with the other dogs. Graynor walked over, put his heavily grayed muzzle into her palm. She gently stroked his face and whispered, "Thank you, boy."

His tail wagged, as he sat beside her, the other dogs milling around. They didn't have the same guard-dog instinct that he did. They were family pets. They would bark if there was something to bark at, but they wouldn't see it ahead of time. At least the guy from her horrible being-followed incident earlier today was now safely caught. At that, she looked up to see Caleb make his way slowly down the stairs. She winced as she saw how stiff he was. "Too bad I don't have a hot tub," she murmured, as he came close, wrapped an arm around her shoulders. He dropped a kiss on her forehead.

"I have to admit that sounds about right for tonight," he said. He watched with her as the intruder was loaded into Ansel's vehicle.

"Is he connected to the one who abused Beowulf?"

"Not only connected but he's also the one who shot the guy at the rental house."

She looked up at him in surprise. "Seriously? He admitted that?"

"More or less. He said it was his cousin, and he didn't have a whole lot of choice, according to him."

"Well, it depends," she said. "Sometimes you just get in so deep that there's no way out."

"And that's partly what this was. Apparently that Huevo guy has kept a grip on this area for a long time, making them do things that nobody was comfortable doing."

"I can believe it."

"So can I," he said. "I saw it with my own eyes today."

"That just makes it way worse," she said. "I'm sorry you had to see it." Gently she wrapped her arms around him and held him carefully. She knew how sore he had to be after that long run. They had only spoken about his injuries once and not so much about his recovery, but she knew that he had both because she'd seen the scars when he took off his shirt at night before sleeping.

And she'd seen the soreness as he tried to move sometimes and didn't quite make it the way he thought he would. Anything that hurt him hurt her. To think about all the suffering he'd already gone through choked her up. And knowing those risks just made it that much harder to let him go off and do whatever he felt he needed to do. But she also knew that to hold the warrior back, like Graynor, she couldn't do that to them. They would feel their lives had no use or no value anymore. She sighed as she watched Ansel and her intruder go. "It's not over though, is it?" she asked Caleb.

"No, not until we get this Huevo guy," he murmured. "There's likely to be an even stronger backlash."

She stiffened at that.

He nodded. "So now I have to consider our plans carefully."

"But will they know where my intruder is, or that he was here?"

"It depends on how rogue this guy is and how well he hid his tracks to make the boss think everything was okay."

"If he was still a trusted employee, maybe Huevo wouldn't watch him as closely?"

"Maybe, but in a case like that, some other guys are always out there, eager to help pull down the others."

"Tattletales?"

"Possibly, and, once the news of the body in the house broke out on the media, it's hard to say just what the boss is feeling like."

Ansel walked back toward them and said, "If you guys have a place to go to for a few days, it would be a good idea," he said. "We'll organize a raid on that compound and take them down," he said, "but it'll take a couple days to set it up. The property lines cross the border giving us some leeway here. And no doubt it needs doing."

"I'd like to be in on that," Caleb said.

Immediately Ansel shook his head. "Can't do that. I understand the sentiment, but you're not part of the team."

"Well, you could make me one," he said in a mild tone.

"No, not without training."

"I've probably had more training than all the guys on your team put together," he said. Ansel looked at him in surprise; Caleb shrugged and gave a little bit of his US Navy SEAL private black-ops history, and he saw Ansel slowly nodding.

"It's not my decision," he said. "It'll have more to do with what the captain sees fit. You're still a civilian in his books."

"Yeah, I am," he said. "But, if you ever needed an extra

set of hands, I know exactly what to do with them."

"Point taken." As he walked back over to the police vehicle, he stopped, turned back, and said, "You know what? If you wanted to go into law enforcement, even if it was like I said, a K9 unit, handling something along that line, you wouldn't need the same physical training the rest of us went through."

"It's possible," he said. "I also have some that might go a long way to convincing the higher-ups."

"Why don't you set up an interview with the captain? See what he has to say."

"I might do that," he said.

Ansel nodded, got into his car, then stopped and said, "Give me a chance to talk to him first."

"That might go a long way to smooth that pathway."

And, with that, he drove off.

"Did he just say he wanted to recommend you for some special training or some special job?"

"I'm not sure he really knew what he was saying," he said in a mild voice. "But I think something was in there."

"And you wanted to go into law enforcement?"

"I want to do something in the same field I've always done, which is similar to that line, yes. A K9 unit wouldn't be a bad idea. I'm not sure that they hire them outside of law enforcement staff though."

"There are so many budget cuts too," she said. "I imagine they probably have a lot of contractors instead."

"And that might not be a bad idea either," he said. "I need a place to do training though, and it takes lots of space for dogs like that."

"Would you do the training for working dogs or for family pets?"

"Both. Every trained dog needs some downtime when he's not working. So they become pets at the same time."

"I like it," she said. "I always wondered if I should be doing more with mine, but that takes time, energy, and dedication. Plus, I didn't have the motivation to take on disciplining four dogs at the same time," she murmured.

"How about taking on one guy now?" he said, tilting her chin up and kissing her gently.

"Well, that motivation is definitely coming along a little bit faster," she said with a laugh. "But, as to the here and now, what will we do about Ansel's suggestion to stay somewhere else a couple nights?"

"I'm not sure," he said. "I don't like the idea of leaving here because, well, we're working on the house, and it's your home, and I think we should defend your own place. I don't want to see us up and running away. But, at the same time, I really don't want you to get hurt."

She rolled her eyes. "I'm fine. And I don't want you hurt any more than you are," she said. "In case you think I didn't notice, I can see how stiffly you're moving."

Caleb just shrugged.

"Well, I vote we stay here," she said. "We won't find any place to take all the animals too."

"I agree," he said, looking down at the dogs milling at their feet. "They should be a pretty good early warning system too."

"Only some of them," she said with a laugh. "I don't delude myself that all of them are that way." She'd bent down and scooped Fancy into her arms. The little Pomeranian immediately licked her chin. "Especially this little one."

Caleb reached over and picked her up and held her against his chest, as she wiggled in delight. "And yet how can you not love her because she's exactly who she's intended to be."

"Exactly, and she is who she really is. She doesn't put on any airs, doesn't try to look any different. She doesn't lie. She doesn't cheat. She is exactly who she is," she murmured, "and I really like that about all my dogs."

"You and me both," he said. "And now I'm starved. And it's very late. I don't know if we'll get a coat on that floor or not," he said, "but it would be better if we did it tonight."

And she groaned and said, "You're a slave driver."

"I am, but it will also take our minds off of everything else happening."

"As long as we don't lose focus," she said.

He looked at her, smiled, and said, "Never."

As they walked back into the kitchen, she said, "I don't know that we have any food though."

"If it is sandwiches, it's sandwiches," he said. He pulled out some sliced meat from the fridge and said, "It looks like sandwiches."

"Since that's ham," she said, "we can do grilled ham and cheese."

And, with that, they set about making enough food for both of them, sat down and ate, then fed the dogs and put on yet more coffee. However, they couldn't sit still and enjoy their coffees.

"I want to get started. And I'm good to drink my coffee cold." He nodded, so they took a few sips and brought their cups upstairs.

She asked, "Same deal as last time? You sand, and I put down the finish?"

"I've got about an hour, an hour and a half left in me," he said, "and then I don't think I can do more."

"Got it. After that, a hot bath for you."

"We are likely not going to have access to the upstairs bathroom for baths. Or just muscle relaxants, maybe even pain pills tonight," he admitted quietly.

She winced, looked at him, and asked, "That bad?"

"Well, it's definitely not good, but I will survive."

With that, they got down to work. He was done within his hour-and-a-half time frame, and, for that, she was grateful. He was looking pretty damn sore, as he slowly moved all the tools back downstairs again. She was in the second bedroom, working away on the coat, when she heard him outside.

She frowned, wondering what she heard, but she had none of the dogs with her—because there was just no way to keep them off the wet finish. As she worked on the upstairs hallway, she couldn't wait for when these upper floors were done. By the time she stopped at the top of the stairs, she sat here, wondering how she kept biting off more than she could chew. It was almost as if her DIY home projects kept her exhausted, so she didn't have to do anything else or maybe not even think about anything else.

And yet she had turned the corner on that too, thinking about her future with Caleb, which was huge for her right now, and it was enough to keep her going. Even if he did go back temporarily to New Mexico, she knew he wouldn't stay there. The more job opportunities there were for him here in El Paso, the better she felt about it all. It was just a matter of him feeling good about it too.

As she walked slowly downstairs, her energy sagging, she saw no sign of him. She looked around, realizing she saw no signs of her dogs either. She then stepped out on the back porch to find him running her four dogs through drills and basically playing and doing training.

He looked up at her, smiled, and walked over.

"I figured you'd be crashed in bed."

"I took some medication," he admitted. "I wanted to give it some time to work. So I took the dogs out to just see how good their training was."

"And how are they?" she murmured, looking down at the happy dogs at his feet.

"Well, a little untrained, a little undisciplined, but obviously happy with their lot in life here," he said with a bright smile.

She looked at him and returned his smile. "It's late," she murmured. "You should be resting."

"That's what I was thinking, but I can't crash if you are still working. I wanted to come up, and, indeed, I called out to see if you were okay, but you were too busy to hear me."

"Well, I'm done now," she said, "and I'm so glad this job is over."

"And it looks amazing," he said. "So proud of you."

"I know. I'm really happy with it. It's just really shitty timing to redo the second story."

"Again, there's never a good time to redo a floor," he said. "It's an inconvenience to everybody living in the house. If you don't live there, haven't moved in yet, then that's a whole different story, but we've got furniture and all kinds of people and dogs traipsing up and down."

"Which reminds me, I didn't put up the barrier at the top of the stairs," she said, "and I've gotta do that. So the dogs don't go up there before it dries."

"We can do that on our way back in," he said, calling the dogs as they headed inside.

She replaced the doggie gate, quickly washed up for the

night, wishing that she'd had access to the upstairs bathroom tonight. She would get a shower in the morning hopefully. "I feel sticky," she murmured.

"I hear you," he said, yawning, sleeping beside her on her temporary bed set up in the living room.

"Go to sleep," she whispered. "We'll talk in the morning."

He closed his eyes, and she just waited, as he slipped into a deep sleep. With the dogs arrayed all around him on the bed and on the floor, she slowly drifted in and out of sleep herself. When she thought she heard a sound, she opened her eyes and slowly sat up. She looked at Graynor, but he was relaxed and calm, and, with that, she trusted that he would keep her safe, and she rolled over and went to sleep.

CALEB WOKE EARLY in the morning, rested. Although a little sore, he felt decent. He rolled over to check out what was happening and saw all three small dogs were on the bed beside Laysha. Graynor was stretched out and sound asleep between the two of them. Graynor was completely undisturbed by anything, and that was a good sign. Caleb looked at his watch to find it was seven in the morning. He smiled, reached over, gently pulled the hair off her face, dropped a kiss on her cheek, and went to put on coffee.

Still just in his boxers, he stepped outside the back door. It was a beautiful morning, the air fresh, and he propped open the door. Graynor, now at his side, headed out, lifted a leg. The other small dogs joined Graynor as well; nobody seemed to be too bothered by anything outside.

Inside, the coffee still dripping, he headed back to check

on her. She was sound asleep, and he leaned over and gave her a gentle kiss, unable to keep from touching her. When she murmured something, he leaned over and asked, "What was that?"

"I missed you," she said, snuggling against his cheek.

"I wasn't gone for long," he murmured.

She opened her eyes, raised her arms, snagged him around his neck, and pulled him down beside her.

He chuckled.

"You were gone," she said. "You were gone a lifetime."

He chuckled. "Only about fifteen minutes."

"Before that."

"No, still not a lifetime," he said, "but over five years and, for that, I'm so damn sorry."

She nodded and nuzzled his neck gently.

He could feel his body instantly responding. "You're playing with fire."

"Any reason not to?" she asked. "I think we're both consenting adults, and we gave a final send-off to your past yesterday."

"You make a good argument," he said, settling in lower. He'd hoped to get to this point but hadn't wanted to push her. They'd been so crazy busy, and he didn't want their first time to be amid—or brought on by—some case of panic either. He nuzzled and gently kissed her lips and then her neck and on down.

"I should have a shower," she said, stretching beneath him.

"Well, I'd say we could both have one together, but you know we really haven't had enough activity to justify one," he said. "Yet."

She chuckled. "Well, I'm sure we can fix that." She wiggled beneath him.

He groaned gently. "You know it's been a long time for me," he murmured.

"No, it hasn't," she said.

"Oh, definitely since before my accident," he said.

"Well, it's been a long time for me too," she said, squeezing him gently. "After the divorce, I just couldn't even begin to go there."

"In that case, it sounds like perfect timing for both of us." And he dropped his lips to hers and kissed her gently, almost an exploratory mission. But she was having nothing to do with that—that could wait for later. She pulled him down, hugging him harder and tighter against her.

"We don't have to rush," he murmured.

"Yeah, we do," she said.

He gently kissed her back.

She continued, "The fact that we might have a little bit longer to play later will just make it that much nicer afterward."

"Well, I'm not going anywhere," he said, "not for a long time."

She smiled, opened her eyes, and said, "Promise?"

"Absolutely," he said. "I figured I'd stay here with you until I could find a place of my own."

"Or you could just stay here with me," she said.

He looked at her and asked, "Are you sure you're ready for that?"

"You mean, a live-in guest? Why not?" she asked. "We're heading that way now."

"But I don't want to push it," he said, protesting.

"I do," she said in all seriousness. "I feel like we've lost so much time already."

He nodded, slowly kissed her gently, and said, "In that case, we'll keep the idea on the table and discuss the pros and cons as we go."

"Sounds good to me," she said. And then she wiggled yet again beneath him. "Not that I meant to distract you, but where were we?"

He gave a burst of laughter and kissed her deeply, feeling their passion rise between them. It had always been there, had always simmered beneath the surface. For whatever damn reason he'd been so blind to what was always in front of him. It was incredibly upsetting now to see what could have been, and, at the same time, he was just grateful that finally they had come to the awareness of where they really belong.

When she slipped a hand inside his boxers, he shuddered in her palm. "Oh, my God," he whispered, trying to control his breathing. His forehead rested against hers, his eyes closed, as she gently explored him.

"Yeah, that's how I feel," she said.

"It's just been …" And he froze.

"I know. I know. I know," she said, and she kissed him passionately, and he felt everything inside him firing way quicker than he wanted to.

He whispered, "I can't slow this down."

"Don't," she said. "I have no intention of it." And she opened her thighs wide, and he wrapped them up high around his hips. He groaned and said, "We're wearing too many clothes for this."

"Well then, you haven't really been paying attention," she murmured on a giggle, and he realized his boxers were around his ankles. He looked at her aghast. And then he chuckled. "You're good at that."

"No," she said. "I just distracted you at the same time."

And she sat up ever-so-slightly and pulled her T-shirt over her head.

He took care of the tiny cotton panties with his big hands, only to rip them. He looked at her and said, "Oops."

"Not a problem," she said, sliding beneath him, wrapping her legs around him again. "I've got lots more."

He grinned, and it wasn't anything he could control when she reached up and pulled him to her again, kissing him passionately. Their tongues gently wound together, as he held her tight against him, not wanting the moment to end, but knowing that he had no choice but to ride the cascade of emotions as they drove them forward, faster and faster. When he finally entered her, it was almost like a homecoming. He stopped for a moment to breathe.

"You feel so damn good," he murmured.

"More than good," she said, panting beneath him. "It feels right."

He agreed. And he plunged deep and then again and again and again. When she came apart in his arms, he never had any feeling quite the same, and he followed her over the edge, almost immediately knowing that she held him safe while he collapsed beside her.

CHAPTER 16

"**W**ELL," LAYSHA MURMURED, "that was worth waiting for."

"Glad to hear it," Caleb said, still gasping for breath. "And a hell of a way to start the morning."

"Now a shower would be perfect," she said and gave him a cheeky grin. "You coming?"

"I'll be up in a minute," he said, and she bounced to her feet, more energized than she'd felt in days. She raced up the stairs, glad to find the floor completely dry, and ran into her shower, hoping he'd join her. When he didn't, she quickly dressed, masking her disappointment, but realizing it didn't really matter. They had lots of time. Making her way downstairs, she realized the house was empty. She frowned, stepped outside, faced a stranger, who held a gun on Caleb.

He had his boxers back on, and that was it. He gave her a warning look.

Ignoring that, she looked at the intruder and glowered. "Wow," she said, "seems like we're just full of these assholes who don't know they should knock."

When the older man—somewhere in his late forties, fifties—smiled at her, she saw the cruelty in his gaze and absolutely nothing nice about him. "So are you the boss Huevo then?"

His eyebrows lifted, and slowly he nodded.

"Good," she said, in a calm voice. Walking closer, as he kept nudging the gun against Caleb's head, she taunted him. "At least you came to do the job yourself, instead of sending another lackey."

"He talked, did he?"

"But you knew he would," she murmured, glaring at him. His eyes were dead, as if he'd lost any vestige of humanity. "Why would you even think to feed men to the dogs?"

"It's cheaper than dog food," he sneered. "And that's all they are. They're no better than the dogs that ate them."

"Is that what you want for yourself?"

"Whatever," he said. "It's not exactly a hardship. You'll die one way or the other," he said. "And it makes a great tool for a fear tactic, doesn't it?"

"Just for cowards." She studied Caleb, seeing that urgent warning in his gaze, not sure what he was worried about. Sure, he knew Laysha well enough to know she'd let her words rip. She just didn't know what else worried him at the moment. She remembered her request to bring down the .22 last night but had no idea if he actually had. They'd been a little sidetracked by everything else that had gone on. She'd looked at Huevo's handgun and looked at the asshole and said, "So you didn't kill us outright. What's your big plan now?"

"Well, I need to know what you guys know," he said, "to see how far the damage runs."

"What the damage is?" she said. "I mean, I already texted the detectives that the compound was empty, and they should be getting their asses over there right now."

He stared at her in shock, jerking the gun.

Somehow she knew Huevo wasn't jerking the gun before

firing off a shot. He exhibited more control than that. She figured he was tempted to aim at her, but his common sense took over, knowing Caleb was the bigger threat. She avoided looking at Caleb because, by now, he knew she was purposely poking the bear here, hoping Huevo would point his gun, his only gun, at her. She knew Caleb would attack at that point.

"You did what?"

She shrugged. "Well, it's not like your men can mount any real resistance there, can they? Not without you present. Your guys are pretty shitty at defending the place."

He glared at her. "You don't know anything about me," he said.

"I know you're wasting time here," she snapped. "While you're here, your men are dealing with the cops."

"Goddammit," he snapped, raising the handgun in her direction.

Immediately Caleb grabbed the gunman's wrist in a vise grip that brought the gunman to his knees, screaming.

She pivoted, hopefully in the right direction to avoid any bullet, and almost thought she heard bones breaking, as Caleb crushed the gunman's hand.

She stepped closer, and, with all her might, she punched Huevo hard in the nose. He cried out again, as he sat down from the force of her blow, his nose now spewing blood. She glared at him. "You're such a fucking asshole," she said. "How could you do that to the dogs?"

He stared at her in bewilderment.

"He doesn't understand," Caleb said, as he twisted the crushed fist behind the gunman's back and pinned him to the floor. "He thought you'd be concerned about the people."

"Well, I am to a certain extent," she said, "but I'm also really pissed that he would turn those animals into that, and now they have to be put down." She looked at Caleb. "You got this guy?" He nodded. She stalked into the kitchen, grabbed zap straps, came back, and they quickly tied his wrists and ankles. "You know what?" she said to Huevo. "You're nothing without the dogs and without that gun."

"You're nothing but a bitch," he said. "When I get out of here, I'll make sure I feed you to the dogs."

"Well, you would if you could, but that ain't going to happen," she said.

He just sneered at her.

She turned toward Caleb. "Why don't we just kill him now?" she asked.

Huevo gasped, surprised again.

She rounded on him. "All talk and bluster, no action. A bully playing army."

Caleb looked up at her with a knowing smirk and said, "I understand the sentiment. Believe me, I do. But we have to follow the law."

"He broke into my house, and he held us at gunpoint."

"And I've already called Ansel."

"Perfect," she said. "Hopefully he can clean up the rest of the garbage around the compound too."

At that, they stood the gunman up and walked him out to the front yard. His feet may have been tethered, but he could take baby steps still. Caleb pointed Huevo's own gun at him, prodding him along.

A series of gunfire erupted, and Caleb threw Laysha to the ground. Just seconds later, the gunman fell to the ground beside them.

She whispered to Caleb, "Now what?"

"I'm not sure, but a guy like that must have an awful lot of enemies."

Laysha lifted her head, seeing a woman standing there, her rifle at her side.

The woman stared at Caleb, raising up on one elbow, holding a gun, pointed at the ground. "You can shoot me if you want, but he took my daughter from me, and he fed her to his damn dogs. My precious child didn't deserve to die. And Huevo didn't deserve to live. I followed him here, knowing it was my one chance."

"And who are you?"

"I was his latest acquisition, not for sex but to look after the dogs, knowing that I would be fed to them next. *Huevo didn't deserve to live.*" At that, she melted into the background.

Caleb looked at Laysha, stood, offering her a hand up.

"She deserves her freedom," Laysha said. "I didn't see anything. Did you?"

He snorted. "I can't identify her, and, if she gets the hell out of here, neither will Ansel."

They heard sirens in the distance. Laysha walked over, looked down at the gunman. "I know they have to destroy those dogs, and I'm so sorry about that," she said, "but I'm really glad this asshole won't do evil to any more dogs or to anybody else."

Caleb wrapped her up in his arms, even as the detective approached, and asked, "What the hell now?" He stopped and stared. "Wow."

"I know," Caleb said. They told him about the woman and what she'd said.

Even the detective winced at that. "Well, I don't know who she is, and I know that what she did was wrong, but personally I won't put too much effort into trying to find her. If she's smart, she'll cross the border and disappear into Mexico," he said quietly. "She has already suffered enough. A guy like this? Well, we didn't want him in the legal system anyway."

"Maybe not," Caleb said, "but we couldn't have done what she did."

"I know. And, to that end, we'll look at how we can take care of the rest of the compound. We're working with the Mexican police on this. His property crosses the border."

"Good, a lot of people died on that property."

"The prisoner is talking," he said. "He won't get free himself, but he's doing what he can to make up for whatever he did."

"I think an awful lot of people were taken down the wrong path because of this asshole," she whispered, kicking the dead body. Just to be sure ...

Ansel grabbed his cell phone and pushed one of his speed-dial numbers. "Get the coroner out here and forensics too." Off the phone now, he approached them. "I've gotta wait here for the team. I'll need your statements. Otherwise go about your day." And Ansel walked off to his vehicle, sitting inside, the door propped open, back on his phone again.

Caleb turned, a fierce frown on his face.

Laysha knew what coming.

"Don't you *ever* do that again."

Had she not known him so well, she would have been scared, his delivery low and lethal. "You weren't surprised. You *knew* what I was doing."

"Never again, Laysha," he said, louder, deeper.

"No."

"Laysha!"

"No, Caleb," she repeated, stepping closer to him, softening her voice. "I will always protect you and my dogs—and my home. You know that. And I know you will always protect me—and my dogs and my home—while protecting yourself as well. So we are all protected." She waited, watched, wondered if he would still be mad.

"I could have lost you," he murmured.

"And I wouldn't want to be here if I lost you."

He reached up a hand, caressed her cheek, and then his phone rang. She raised her eyebrows as he pulled it out and said, "It's the vet."

She smiled. "And?"

He put it on Speakerphone. The vet's voice was jubilant. "Beowulf had a great night," he said, "and he's looking forward to coming home."

She cried out with joy. She looked over at Caleb. "Shall we go get him now?"

He nodded. "You did hear," he said with a big grin, as he put away his phone, "the vet said *come home*, right?"

"I know, and that's what it is. This is home for the War Dog." She kissed Caleb hard and bailed to gather her dogs, while Caleb informed Ansel where they were off to.

She had all four of her dogs in the back of the truck by the time Caleb joined her now fully dressed. "We have to get permission to keep him," he said.

"Not a problem," she said. "You'll make it happen."

He gave her a shadow of laughter. "I don't know about that."

"Well, we have a vet bill to pay, and we have another animal to look after, and a floor to finish," she said. "And that's just today."

He rolled his eyes. "You and that floor."

"Well, considering that we have other jobs and other projects," she said, "and I now have a semipermanent houseguest, you know the floor is important."

"*Semi?*" He laughed. "We need to discuss that part further. I expect to be *permanently* here. With you."

Now she chuckled.

They got to the vet's, opened the front door, and, as they waited in the reception room, the vet slowly brought out Beowulf. As soon as the dogs saw Beowulf, they all raced over to him. She tried to call them back, but Graynor walked over gently and then slowly turned around and walked at the same pace as the injured dog as they came toward Caleb, matching slow stride for slow stride.

Caleb crouched, and Beowulf immediately walked right into his arms. Laysha could feel the tears choking the back of her throat, as she watched the two of them bond like she knew she probably never could. But to know that Caleb had saved this animal's life? Well, that just made her fall in love with Caleb all that much more again. When Beowulf lifted his head, Caleb turned, looked at her, and held out a hand. "Meet the newest member of the family."

She sat down beside Beowulf and waited. The dog slowly inched closer and dropped his head on her lap and just looked up at her with the soulful eyes of a damn grateful animal. She gently caressed his ears and whispered, "You'll be fine now, buddy, absolutely fine."

She looked up at the vet with tears in her eyes, and she whispered, "Thank you."

He nodded. "And no charge for a War Dog," he said. "This animal deserves everything good coming his way. He has seen the worst and the best in humanity. Let's hope it's only the best from now on."

She smiled and said, "You can count on it from our part. Only the best for all of us," she said, as she was surrounded by her dog family and Caleb. She'd never felt happier; she looked over at Caleb and said, "Right?"

He leaned over, kissed her, and said, "Absolutely. Now we'll work on our wedding plans and see who to invite." She opened her mouth, but no words came out. "Absolutely not Jackson. Not Sarah. No argument."

She grinned and said, "Five dogs for sure, so that means the wedding is at home."

And he burst out laughing, with the vet and Sandy grinning madly. He gave her another lingering kiss. "Anything you want, sweetie. I'm totally okay with it."

And she knew that her life had taken a turn she had never anticipated and was damn grateful for it. She gave each of her dogs a cuddle and a kiss. They all seemed to understand something wonderful had just happened, and the smaller dogs danced around. The older, bigger two seemed to smile at her. She smiled back, stood up, and said, "Come on. It's time to go home."

And there were never any better words to be found in the dictionary.

EPILOGUE

Kurt Manchester walked into Badger's office. "Wow," he said. "I don't know what to do with this. You actually have an office of your own."

Badger looked up, grinned, and said, "Kat insisted. Otherwise I leave my shit everywhere."

Kurt laughed, sat down on the nearest chair, and said, "What did you want to see me about?"

"Well, I'm sure you've heard about the War Dogs that we've been dealing with," he said, one eyebrow lifted as he looked at Kurt.

Kurt nodded. "Yeah, heard something about it. You're almost done with those, aren't you?"

"Nope, not happening apparently," he said. "We've got another half dozen here anyway. I haven't even counted them but was trying to finish off the original files. And this is the last of them," he said. "When the department went to check up on it, the adoptees admitted that they had only done the adoption for the husband's brother because he'd really, really wanted it. But, when they followed up with the brother, he had taken off, and the dog was nowhere to be found."

"And now?"

"We found the brother. He's in jail."

"Wow," he said, "so where the hell is the dog?"

"The brother has no idea, says that the dog never adjusted well to being there, and wasn't exactly friendly, so he didn't really give a shit."

"Great, and what did he do?"

"He gave her to a trucker."

"Well, that's still not necessarily bad news," he said. "A trucker would probably enjoy the dog and keep her on long hauls."

"Yep, until he got to Kentucky," he said. "And he lost the dog."

"Okay," Kurt said, slowly getting an idea. "And that's why you're asking me?"

"Well, Kentucky is your home state, isn't it?"

"Yes," he said. "But how long ago was the dog lost there?"

"We were given the file awhile ago," he said. "And we did look at all these, and we found no good leads on any of them. So we weren't in too much of a panic to put too many man-hours in this direction. We've done the best footwork we can, but this is the oldest one we've got."

"So that's a really cold case for me to look after," he said, reaching for the file. He opened it up to a picture of a completely golden not-quite-shepherd-looking Malinois. "So definitely female," he said, guessing from the size.

"Yes, she's female. She's fixed. She was an excellent War Dog. She was an IED-sniffing, bomb-sniffing dog, and she was really good at sniffing out the enemy's weapons in hidden corners. She's an expert at hiding herself and has done a ton of outdoor training. Her name is Sabine."

"In other words, she'll see the world as her enemy. She won't know who to trust, and she spent these last weeks living on her own."

"Maybe," he said, "and I know you think the department was derelict in not getting into this earlier, but we did contact several people that we know throughout the state of Kentucky where the trucker was, where Sabine was last seen, and yesterday we got a tip, saying that somebody had seen a dog looking just like this one at a truck stop."

"Would it be likely that she'd still be there?"

"The only thing we could think of is it's the last place that she had human contact. And remember. She's five, and she's spent quite a bit of time with people."

"And was the tip a good tip or a bad tip?"

"That's where the problem comes in," he said. "The tipster said that Sabine was trying to attack people. They'd called animal control, but so far nobody had seen Sabine since."

"I'm on my way," he said, jumping to his feet, clutching the file.

"Wait," Badger said. "We can't pay for this. We'll cover your expenses, but there's no wages."

"That's fine," he said. "Any dog that's been through military training deserves a few good years afterward. It sounds like she's been given a short shrift this time."

"It happens," Badger said, "hopefully not too often. Do you have any K9 training?"

"Maybe not like you mean," he said, "but I've certainly been around dogs all my life. My dad bred them. At least when he was sober enough. My foster families usually had them, for easier assimilation, yada, yada."

"Good enough," he said, "this one could be dangerous."

"She could be," he said, "but maybe it's about time somebody went to find her, intending to rescue her," he said, "instead of capturing her." And with that, Kurt walked out.

This concludes Book 11 of The K9 Files: Caleb.
Read about Kurt: The K9 Files, Book 12

THE K9 FILES: KURT (BOOK #12)

Welcome to the all new K9 Files series reconnecting readers with the unforgettable men from SEALs of Steel in a new series of action packed, page turning romantic suspense that fans have come to expect from USA TODAY Bestselling author Dale Mayer. Pssst... you'll meet other favorite characters from SEALs of Honor and Heroes for Hire too!

Being a badass growing up had been fine for a while, but Kurt knew his life had to change. His best option? The US Navy. Thirteen years later a serendipitous request from Badger to check out reports of a missing War Dog hidden in the bushes and attacking people sends Kurt to the very place he couldn't wait to get out of.

When Kurt chose the navy over Laurie Ann so long ago, he left her with a gift she'd fought long and hard to keep. Plus she didn't give up on her dream of becoming a doctor. When Kurt returns, it's hard not to see the same person she'd loved in this older version. Yet the town has a long memory, and at least one person isn't willing to see who

Kurt is now.

But, as always, he's a trouble magnet. Was he capable of handling the nightmare they were in, or would he leave, just like he had last time?

Find Book 12 here!

To find out more visit Dale Mayer's website.

http://smarturl.it/DMSKurt

Author's Note

Thank you for reading Caleb: The K9 Files, Book 11! If you enjoyed the book, please take a moment and leave a short review.

Dear reader,

I love to hear from readers, and you can contact me at my website: www.dalemayer.com or at my Facebook author page. To be informed of new releases and special offers, sign up for my newsletter or follow me on BookBub. And if you are interested in joining Dale Mayer's Reader Group, here is the Facebook sign up page.

https://smarturl.it/DaleMayerFBGroup

Cheers,
Dale Mayer

Get THREE Free Books Now!

Have you met the SEALS of Honor?

SEALs of Honor Books 1, 2, and 3. Follow the stories of brave, badass warriors who serve their country with honor and love their women to the limits of life and death.

Read Mason, Hawk, and Dane right now for FREE.

Go here and tell me where to send them!
http://smarturl.it/EthanBofB

About the Author

Dale Mayer is a USA Today bestselling author best known for her Psychic Visions and Family Blood Ties series. Her contemporary romances are raw and full of passion and emotion (Second Chances, SKIN), her thrillers will keep you guessing (By Death series), and her romantic comedies will keep you giggling (It's a Dog's Life and Charmin Marvin Romantic Comedy series).

She honors the stories that come to her – and some of them are crazy and break all the rules and cross multiple genres!

To go with her fiction, she also writes nonfiction in many different fields with books available on resume writing, companion gardening and the US mortgage system. She has recently published her Career Essentials Series. All her books are available in print and ebook format.

Connect with Dale Mayer Online

Dale's Website – www.dalemayer.com
Facebook Personal – https://smarturl.it/DaleMayerFacebook
Instagram – https://smarturl.it/DaleMayerInstagram
BookBub – https://smarturl.it/DaleMayerBookbub
Facebook Fan Page – https://smarturl.it/DaleMayerFBFanPage
Goodreads – https://smarturl.it/DaleMayerGoodreads

Also by Dale Mayer

Published Adult Books:

Hathaway House
Aaron, Book 1
Brock, Book 2
Cole, Book 3
Denton, Book 4
Elliot, Book 5
Finn, Book 6
Gregory, Book 7
Heath, Book 8
Iain, Book 9
Jaden, Book 10
Keith, Book 11
Lance, Book 12
Melissa, Book 13
Nash, Book 14
Owen, Book 15
Hathaway House, Books 1–3
Hathaway House, Books 4–6
Hathaway House, Books 7–9

The K9 Files
Ethan, Book 1
Pierce, Book 2
Zane, Book 3

Blaze, Book 4
Lucas, Book 5
Parker, Book 6
Carter, Book 7
Weston, Book 8
Greyson, Book 9
Rowan, Book 10
Caleb, Book 11
Kurt, Book 12

Lovely Lethal Gardens
Arsenic in the Azaleas, Book 1
Bones in the Begonias, Book 2
Corpse in the Carnations, Book 3
Daggers in the Dahlias, Book 4
Evidence in the Echinacea, Book 5
Footprints in the Ferns, Book 6
Gun in the Gardenias, Book 7
Handcuffs in the Heather, Book 8
Ice Pick in the Ivy, Book 9
Jewels in the Juniper, Book 10
Killer in the Kiwis, Book 11
Lovely Lethal Gardens, Books 1–2
Lovely Lethal Gardens, Books 3–4
Lovely Lethal Gardens, Books 5–6
Lovely Lethal Gardens, Books 7–8
Lovely Lethal Gardens, Books 9–10

Psychic Vision Series
Tuesday's Child
Hide 'n Go Seek
Maddy's Floor

Garden of Sorrow
Knock Knock…
Rare Find
Eyes to the Soul
Now You See Her
Shattered
Into the Abyss
Seeds of Malice
Eye of the Falcon
Itsy-Bitsy Spider
Unmasked
Deep Beneath
From the Ashes
Stroke of Death
Ice Maiden
Psychic Visions Books 1–3
Psychic Visions Books 4–6
Psychic Visions Books 7–9

By Death Series
Touched by Death
Haunted by Death
Chilled by Death
By Death Books 1–3

Broken Protocols – Romantic Comedy Series
Cat's Meow
Cat's Pajamas
Cat's Cradle
Cat's Claus
Broken Protocols 1-4

Broken and... Mending
Skin
Scars
Scales (of Justice)
Broken but... Mending 1-3

Glory
Genesis
Tori
Celeste
Glory Trilogy

Biker Blues
Morgan: Biker Blues, Volume 1
Cash: Biker Blues, Volume 2

SEALs of Honor
Mason: SEALs of Honor, Book 1
Hawk: SEALs of Honor, Book 2
Dane: SEALs of Honor, Book 3
Swede: SEALs of Honor, Book 4
Shadow: SEALs of Honor, Book 5
Cooper: SEALs of Honor, Book 6
Markus: SEALs of Honor, Book 7
Evan: SEALs of Honor, Book 8
Mason's Wish: SEALs of Honor, Book 9
Chase: SEALs of Honor, Book 10
Brett: SEALs of Honor, Book 11
Devlin: SEALs of Honor, Book 12
Easton: SEALs of Honor, Book 13
Ryder: SEALs of Honor, Book 14
Macklin: SEALs of Honor, Book 15

Corey: SEALs of Honor, Book 16
Warrick: SEALs of Honor, Book 17
Tanner: SEALs of Honor, Book 18
Jackson: SEALs of Honor, Book 19
Kanen: SEALs of Honor, Book 20
Nelson: SEALs of Honor, Book 21
Taylor: SEALs of Honor, Book 22
Colton: SEALs of Honor, Book 23
Troy: SEALs of Honor, Book 24
Axel: SEALs of Honor, Book 25
Baylor: SEALs of Honor, Book 26
SEALs of Honor, Books 1–3
SEALs of Honor, Books 4–6
SEALs of Honor, Books 7–10
SEALs of Honor, Books 11–13
SEALs of Honor, Books 14–16
SEALs of Honor, Books 17–19
SEALs of Honor, Books 20–22
SEALs of Honor, Books 23–25

Heroes for Hire
Levi's Legend: Heroes for Hire, Book 1
Stone's Surrender: Heroes for Hire, Book 2
Merk's Mistake: Heroes for Hire, Book 3
Rhodes's Reward: Heroes for Hire, Book 4
Flynn's Firecracker: Heroes for Hire, Book 5
Logan's Light: Heroes for Hire, Book 6
Harrison's Heart: Heroes for Hire, Book 7
Saul's Sweetheart: Heroes for Hire, Book 8
Dakota's Delight: Heroes for Hire, Book 9
Michael's Mercy (Part of Sleeper SEAL Series)
Tyson's Treasure: Heroes for Hire, Book 10

Jace's Jewel: Heroes for Hire, Book 11
Rory's Rose: Heroes for Hire, Book 12
Brandon's Bliss: Heroes for Hire, Book 13
Liam's Lily: Heroes for Hire, Book 14
North's Nikki: Heroes for Hire, Book 15
Anders's Angel: Heroes for Hire, Book 16
Reyes's Raina: Heroes for Hire, Book 17
Dezi's Diamond: Heroes for Hire, Book 18
Vince's Vixen: Heroes for Hire, Book 19
Ice's Icing: Heroes for Hire, Book 20
Johan's Joy: Heroes for Hire, Book 21
Galen's Gemma: Heroes for Hire, Book 22
Zack's Zest: Heroes for Hire, Book 23
Heroes for Hire, Books 1–3
Heroes for Hire, Books 4–6
Heroes for Hire, Books 7–9
Heroes for Hire, Books 10–12
Heroes for Hire, Books 13–15

SEALs of Steel
Badger: SEALs of Steel, Book 1
Erick: SEALs of Steel, Book 2
Cade: SEALs of Steel, Book 3
Talon: SEALs of Steel, Book 4
Laszlo: SEALs of Steel, Book 5
Geir: SEALs of Steel, Book 6
Jager: SEALs of Steel, Book 7
The Final Reveal: SEALs of Steel, Book 8
SEALs of Steel, Books 1–4
SEALs of Steel, Books 5–8
SEALs of Steel, Books 1–8

The Mavericks
Kerrick, Book 1
Griffin, Book 2
Jax, Book 3
Beau, Book 4
Asher, Book 5
Ryker, Book 6
Miles, Book 7
Nico, Book 8
Keane, Book 9
Lennox, Book 10
Gavin, Book 11
Shane, Book 12

Bullard's Battle Series
Ryland's Reach, Book 1
Cain's Cross, Book 2
Eton's Escape, Book 3
Garret's Gambit, Book 4
Kano's Keep, Book 5
Fallon's Flaw, Book 6
Quinn's Quest, Book 7
Bullard's Beauty, Book 8

Collections
Dare to Be You…
Dare to Love…
Dare to be Strong…
RomanceX3

Standalone Novellas
It's a Dog's Life

Riana's Revenge
Second Chances

Published Young Adult Books:

Family Blood Ties Series
Vampire in Denial
Vampire in Distress
Vampire in Design
Vampire in Deceit
Vampire in Defiance
Vampire in Conflict
Vampire in Chaos
Vampire in Crisis
Vampire in Control
Vampire in Charge
Family Blood Ties Set 1–3
Family Blood Ties Set 1–5
Family Blood Ties Set 4–6
Family Blood Ties Set 7–9
Sian's Solution, A Family Blood Ties Series Prequel Novelette

Design series
Dangerous Designs
Deadly Designs
Darkest Designs
Design Series Trilogy

Standalone
In Cassie's Corner
Gem Stone (a Gemma Stone Mystery)

Published Non-Fiction Books:

Career Essentials
Career Essentials: The Résumé
Career Essentials: The Cover Letter
Career Essentials: The Interview
Career Essentials: 3 in 1

Made in the USA
Columbia, SC
01 March 2021